Copyright © 2(

All rights reserved

The characters and events portrayed in this book are fictitious. Any similarity to real persons, living or dead, is coincidental and not intended by the author.

No part of this book may be reproduced, or stored in a retrieval system, or transmitted in any form or by any means, electronic, mechanical, photocopying, recording, or otherwise, without express written permission of the publisher.

Cover design by: Craig Zerf

CONTENTS

Copyright

Earth's RPG Overlords   1

Chapter 1   2

Chapter 2   9

Chapter 3   17

Chapter 4   25

Chapter 5   33

Chapter 6   39

Chapter 7   45

Chapter 8   58

Chapter 9   63

Chapter 10   75

Chapter 11   82

Chapter 12   90

Chapter 13   94

Chapter 14   103

Chapter 15   110

Chapter 16	119
Chapter 17	127
Chapter 18	132
Chapter 19	136
Chapter 20	146
Chapter 21	151
Chapter 22	160
Chapter 23	167
Chapter 24	178
Chapter 25	187
Chapter 26	196
Chapter 27	203
Chapter 28	207
Chapter 29	211
Chapter 30	222
Chapter 31	230
Chapter 32	236
Chapter 33	250
Chapter 34	253

EARTH'S RPG OVERLORDS
Book 2 - EXPANSION
An Earth Apocalypse System Integration LitRPG Adventure novel

CHAPTER 1

Cash Stone stood on the watchtower, his cybernetic arm resting on the cold stone parapet as he surveyed the city below. The wind rustled his hair. His stormy blue eyes held a melancholy gaze, betraying a lifetime of suffering and loss. Cash was a grizzled, battle-scarred former soldier, a reluctant hero who never wanted the spotlight, but had it thrust upon him.

"Fuck me sideways," he mumbled under his breath, taking in the small but well upgraded town of Tomahawk, now considered to be a Capital City by the System and its douchebag Overlords. "What have I gotten myself into?"

At his feet, Bonny, his loyal Tamaskan dog, wagged her bushy tail, her golden eyes flicking towards her master with concern. She let out a soft whine, sensing his unease. Cash patted her head, a slight smile tugging at the corner of his mouth. "Relax, girl. It's just another day in paradise."

The transformation of Tomahawk from a broken collection of buildings, inhabited by townsfolk who had been under the dire control of a Boss mob and its evil artifact, to a Capital City had been nothing short of miraculous. Cash had used a bunch of his hard-earned System Points to achieve the transformation. He'd constructed massive stone walls, complete with watch towers and a large gate, and topped with giant scorpion crossbows and catapults. Then he had installed mana driven electrical power, an efficient water system, and upgraded accommodation for all.

"Nothing says 'I'm fucking serious' like ten-foot-thick stone walls," Cash said to himself, cracking his knuckles.

In the city center, he had erected a Lord's residence for himself, though he loathed the idea of living like royalty. The imposing structure towered over the surrounding buildings, serving as a symbol of his leadership, much to his chagrin. He'd also created a Crafting Hall, where artisans and craftsmen could hone their skills, producing weapons, armor, and other vital supplies for the city's inhabitants.

And finally, a System Registered shop, where one could sell loot, purchase spells, skills and upgrades. All of this had been necessary to enable the town to be classed as a Capital City. A moniker Cash thought ridiculous when one considered there were only a few hundred people in the town. Which hardly made it a city.

"Great," Cash muttered sarcastically. "Now I've done all that, they'll probably expect me to cut ribbons and shit. Didn't sign up for this clusterfuck," he grumbled, adjusting the straps of his armor. "But what choice did I have, these idiots would have all become monster shit if I hadn't done something."

Bonny nudged her wet nose against his hand, her eyes filled with understanding. She had been by his side through it all, her keen senses and unwavering loyalty serving as a beacon of hope in even the darkest of times.

"Alright, girl," Cash said, casting one last glance over the city. "Enough whining and complaining, let's get back to work."

Before Cash could leave the wall, Sarah appeared, her standard half-grin on her face, radiating her usual upbeat aura. "Hey mister fancy-pants, lord and master," she teased. "What's with the scowly face?"

"Didn't ask for this, Sarah. What do I know about being a leader?" Cash said, his cybernetic hand clenching in frustration. "I built myself a Lord's residence. I'm sorta embarrassed about that. I come from a one room cabin in the woods, now I got a massive mansion. Bloody hell, this is getting so outa hand."

"Take it easy, Cash," Sarah said, her hand resting on his shoulder. "You've done more than anyone could've expected, you deserve a nice place. Hey, and I get to stay in it as well, can't say it bothers me like it does you. And bear in mind, you also raised a Crafting Hall for the people."

"Right, because nothing says 'hope' like

crafting weapons of war," Cash snorted. "And that System Shop? Feels like a damn cheat code."

"Maybe so," Sarah admitted, "but it's the edge we need in this new world. Look, you agreed to stay here for a bit, Cash. To use Tomahawk as your base of operations." She locked eyes with him, determination shining in her gaze. "You've got a gift, and you're exactly what these people need."

"Fuck," Cash sighed, rubbing his temples. "Fine, I'll stay. But don't expect me to wear a crown or hold court. I'm no Lord Appalachia."

"Actually, that is exactly what you are," grinned Sarah, her smile infectious. "Now, let's get to work, and try to be nice," she stressed. "Or at least, less scary than usual."

"Christ, I'm no fucking diplomat," Cash muttered as he surveyed the bustling streets of Tomahawk. "I'm just a soldier." People were going about their daily tasks, the air filled with determination and hope. It was a far cry from the desolate town they had stumbled upon not so long ago.

"Which is precisely why they need you, sir," chimed in Higgins, the AI assistant provided to Cash by the System. "You've already proven your ability to fortify this city and provide for its inhabitants."

"Right, because I excel at turning shit into gold," Cash said, sarcasm dripping from his words. He clenched his fists involuntarily, feeling the smooth metal of his prosthetics against his skin.

Years of being a crippled recluse had taken their toll on him, making the idea of leading a whole town seem ludicrous.

"Indeed, your unique perspective and skill set are invaluable in these trying times," Higgins replied, his snarky British accent somehow both comforting and infuriating.

"Fine, fine." Cash relented, sighing. "But I swear, if any of these people start looking at me like I'm some kind of god, I'll lose my shit."

"Understood, sir," Higgins said, his digital voice tinged with amusement. "Would you like me to begin preparations for a meeting with the townsfolk? You need to select some sort of governing committee. Perhaps we can discuss strategies for maintaining order and addressing any potential threats."

"Ugh, council meetings?" Cash groaned. "What's next, taxes and tithes? Fucking kill me now."

"Sir, your distaste for bureaucracy is duly noted," Higgins replied dryly. "However, effective management and organization are key to ensuring the continued growth of Tomahawk."

"Alright, alright," Cash grumbled, rubbing his temples. "Set up the damn meeting. But if anyone even mentions the word 'politics,' I'm out."

"Very well, sir," Higgins confirmed, a hint of satisfaction in his synthetic voice as the team entered Cash's residence.

Cash traipsed up the grand staircase and stood

on the main balcony, allowing himself a moment to take in the view.

"Fuck me," he murmured, shaking his head. "I never thought I'd be doing this."

"Life is full of surprises, Mr. Stone," Higgins quipped. "Now, if you'll excuse me, I have a council meeting to arrange."

"Fine," Cash said, turning away from the view. "But remember, no politics. If I wanted that shit, I'd watch cable news. Not that it exists anymore."

"Of course, sir," Higgins replied, his digital chuckle fading as he set about his task.

Cash sighed. The truth was, leading Tomahawk had forced Cash to confront parts of himself he had long buried. His military training and cybernetic enhancements had come in handy, but they had also reminded him of the sacrifices he had made – friends lost, limbs replaced, dreams shattered.

"Being a leader isn't easy, is it?" he mused, running a hand through his hair.

"No shit," agreed Sarah. "But you're doing okay, Cash."

"Thanks, Sarah," Cash said, his gaze fixed on the horizon. "But sometimes I can't help but wonder... have I done enough?"

"Only time will tell," she replied. "But one thing is certain – the people of Tomahawk are better off with you at their side."

"Maybe," Cash conceded, a small smile tugging at the corners of his mouth as he looked down at

Bonny, who had fallen asleep. "Just maybe."

CHAPTER 2

Cash stood in the center of the town square, his cybernetic limbs humming faintly as he scanned the sea of faces before him. He could feel the weight of their collective expectations pressing down upon him like a heavy fog. Higgins had called for a general town meeting, and now it was time for Cash to decide who would form the new town council.

"Alright, listen up!" Cash barked, projecting his voice through the crisp autumn air. "I know I ain't much for speeches, but I need y'all to bear with me. We're gonna choose our town council today, and I want people who ain't afraid to speak their minds and get shit done. No kiss-ass, brown-nosing crap that you probably had to do when mayor moustache was in charge."

The crowd murmured their agreement and a couple chuckled out loud. Cash felt a slight twinge of relief. At least they were on board with his vision for a more honest and effective leadership.

"First things first," Cash said, his eyes scanning

the faces before finally landing on Greta. "Greta, step forward."

The crowd parted to reveal Greta, the woman who had famously punched the previous mayor right in the kisser when he had tried to make a one-sided deal with Cash, asking for help but giving nothing in return. She raised an eyebrow at Cash, her hands on her hips, defiance etched into every line of her face.

"Me?" she asked, her voice laced with suspicion. "What do you want with me, Lord Cash?"

Cash allowed himself a small smirk as he replied, "Firstly, just Cash. No Lord. Well, Greta, I reckon you've got some serious balls to punch the mayor like that. And if there's one thing I need in my council, it's someone with the guts to stand up and tell me when I'm being a goddamn idiot."

A ripple of laughter coursed through the assembled townsfolk, and Greta couldn't help but grudgingly smile as well. "Fine," she said, crossing her arms over her chest. "But if I'm gonna do this, you better believe I won't hesitate to call you out on your bullshit."

"Deal," Cash said, extending his right hand for Greta to shake. She eyed it warily but took it in her own, her grip firm and unyielding.

"Alright then, folks," Cash announced, turning back to the audience. "I've made my first choice - Greta here is gonna be my right-hand woman. Now let's see who else we can find to whip this town into shape."

As the crowd began to throw out suggestions and nominees, Cash felt a strange sense of optimism take root within him. Maybe, just maybe, with Greta by his side, he'd stand a chance at building a council that was actually worth a damn.

"Get ready, Tomahawk," he muttered under his breath. "Shit's about to change around here."

With the town meeting winding down and the sun sinking low in the sky, Cash and Greta found themselves seated on a pair of battered folding chairs, poring over a list of potential advisors. Greta's eyes flicked across the names, her brow furrowing as she considered each candidate.

"First things first," Greta began, tapping her finger against a name on the list. "You'll need someone who knows their way around agriculture. We've got to keep the food supply stable, or this whole place goes to shit."

Cash nodded in agreement, his cybernetic hand scratching at his scruffy beard. "Got anyone in mind?"

"Martha," Greta replied without hesitation. "Old lady knows more about farming than anyone else in this town. She's stubborn as hell, but if you can get her on board, she'll make sure we're fed."

"Martha it is," Cash said, scribbling a note beside her name.

"Next up, medical expertise. We're gonna have our hands full keeping people alive with all the crazy shit that comes our way." Greta scanned the list, her lips pursed in thought. "What about Doc Simmons? He's been patching us up for years."

"Simmons, huh?" Cash mused. "Yeah, if you say so. Let's add him to the roster. We also need a strong man, or woman, don't give a shit. You know, to be in charge of security, a town guard, maybe even some sort of police force."

"I know what you mean," acknowledged Greta. "Someone who knows how to keep people in line and focused when things go sideways," she paused, her gaze settling on a name near the bottom of the list. "I've heard stories about this Jonnie Parker guy, a former Marine Gunnery Sergeant. Sounds like he could whip this town into shape."

"Jonnie, huh?" Cash's eyes narrowed. "A Marine? And a Gunny?" Cash chuckled. "Fucking crayon eater. No, but seriously, any Marine is good enough for me. Put him on the list."

"Good," Greta said, nodding decisively. "Also, here, Tom Park, he used to be the town librarian, great at organizing shit. Peter Mason, accountant, could be good for logistics and such. I can't think of exact positions for them, but I know they're good at getting stuff done, and they don't have giant sized egos."

"Nice, tack them on the list as well," agreed Cash. "That's a solid start. We can fill in the gaps later, but these folks should give us a fighting chance at keeping this place together."

"Cool, I'll inform them all that they just

volunteered to be part of the town council," said Greta.

"Thanks, Greta," Cash said, feeling a swell of gratitude towards the no-nonsense woman beside him. "Couldn't have done this without you."

"Damn right," Greta replied with a snort, her eyes twinkling with amusement. "Just remember, you asked for my help. So don't come crying to me when I tell you your ideas are fucking stupid."

"Wouldn't dream of it," Cash chuckled, raising his hands in mock surrender.

As the pair continued to discuss the future of Tomahawk and its council, Cash couldn't help but feel a sense of hope blossoming within him. With Greta's guidance and a team of capable advisors, maybe they really could build something better from the ashes of the old world.

"Get ready, Tomahawk," he thought, a fierce determination burning in his chest. "We're just getting started."

"Hey, Cash," Sarah called out, approaching as Greta walked away. "You know you've got the authority to assign ranks to your vassals, right? Higgins just told me."

Cash raised an eyebrow, his interest piqued. "Really? That might be useful." He mulled it over for a moment, seeing how it could add a sense of order and structure to their newly-formed council.

"Damn straight," Sarah interjected, leaning against a nearby wall. "It's about time we get this motley crew organized."

"Alright, then," Cash said, clapping his hands together with a grin. He paused dramatically as he called up his HUD and inspected some of the names on the long list. Then he swept his arm out toward his friend. "I, Lord Appalachia, do hereby decree that one, Sarah Connor ... shall henceforth be known as Lady Sarah."

"Ha! Very funny," Sarah scoffed, rolling her eyes. Just as she was about to retort, The System chimed in with its robotic voice, announcing her new title.

Title granted: Lady Sarah, Noble of Tomahawk.
May she bring enlightenment and beauty to the position.
All hail Lady Sarah of Tomahawk.

"See?" Cash said triumphantly, even though he was actually a little shocked that his jokey response had been taken seriously by the System. "Even The RPG douche canoe Lords agree with me."

"Holy crap," Sarah conceded, shaking her head with a chuckle. "I suppose there are worse titles I could have."

"Damn right," Cash chimed in, his grin broadening. "At least you didn't get stuck with 'Lord High Protector of Shits Creek' or something equally ridiculous."

"True," Sarah agreed, shuddering at the thought. "I'll take Lady Sarah any day over that."

As Cash and Sarah exchanged banter, Greta returned. "Okay," she interjected. "I told them all that they just volunteered to a seat on the council. On the whole they're fine with that, but you obviously gonna need to talk to them personally. Particularly Gunny, he can be a bit pedantic." Greta turned to Sarah. "So, do I gotta curtsey to you now, or something? Lady Sarah, man, that's weird."

"No need to treat me any different now I am a noble," joshed Sarah. "The odd genuflection, a few deep bows and make sure you address me as, Lady muck-a-muck, and make me tea whenever I demand it."

Greta chuckled. "Yeah, in your dreams."

"Alright, let's get the rest of these folks sorted out," Cash said, scratching his stubbled chin thoughtfully. "Greta, I hereby appoint you as Senior Advisor." Cash announced, trying to sound official but failing to suppress a grin.

"Senior Advisor, huh?" Greta raised an eyebrow, the corner of her mouth tugging up into a smile. "Does that come with any perks? A fancy hat, perhaps?"

"Maybe just a kick in the ass when you need it," Cash retorted, chuckling. "But seriously, your job is to keep me from making dumb decisions, offer honest advice, and manage any conflicts that might arise within our team. You're also going to be my right hand, so you'll have a certain level of authority over the others."

"Understood," Greta nodded solemnly, though her eyes still danced with amusement. "I promise to wield my power responsibly—unless you piss me off, of course."

"Wouldn't dream of it," Cash shot back, his cybernetic arm flexing. He glanced over at Sarah, who had been unusually quiet since being dubbed Lady Sarah. She was staring into the distance, a small, secretive smile playing on her lips. "Hey, Lady Sarah, don't let that title go to your head now."

"Wha—oh, no. Of course not," Sarah stammered, snapping out of her reverie. Cash could tell she was secretly enjoying her new moniker, and it warmed him to see her taking pride in her role. Tomahawk needed people like Sarah—those who were willing to put their skills to good use for the betterment of the town.

"Gunny is gonna be, Security Advisor. Martha, Agricultural Advisor. The rest, let's just go with Advisor's for now, except the Doc. I think I'm gonna call him Head Healer," ended Cash.

"Works for me," agreed Greta.

Sarah nodded.

"Arf!" added Bonny.

CHAPTER 3

Cash Stone, known to the people of Tomahawk as Lord Appalachia, strode through the open heavy oak doors of his residence, determination etched into his face. The grand hall stretched before him, an imposing space filled with dark wood, polished flagstones, and the echoes of decisions yet to be made.

"Alright, let's get this shitshow started," Cash grumbled to himself as he approached the long table where his new advisors waited.

"Ah, Lord Appalachia!" Lady Sarah greeted him with a mischievous grin, as she curtsied with an exaggerated flourish. "Ready to boss us around?"

"Always, Lady Sarah," Cash replied, lips curling into a smirk. "I'd miss it if you didn't give me some sass."

"Good morning, Lord Appalachia," Senior Advisor Greta said, with no sign of sass.

"Greetings all," Cash quipped as he totally

ignored the gilt throne at then head of the table. After all, the System had provided it unasked for, and Cash thought it was ridiculous. Instead he pulled up a normal chair, sat down and drummed his cybernetic fingers nervously on the tabletop.

"Lord Appalachia," Gunny the Security Advisor rumbled in greeting, his sturdy frame radiating authority. "We've got a lot to cover today."

"Indeed we do," Cash agreed, nodding to Martha the Agricultural Advisor, who smiled warmly from beneath her straw hat. "And with your expertise, our food supply will thrive."

"Thank you, Lord Appalachia," Martha replied, her cheeks flushing pink with pride.

"Tom Park, Peter Mason," Cash acknowledged the two remaining advisors with a brief nod. "Your skills will be invaluable in the days ahead."

"Always at your service, Lord Appalachia," Tom replied earnestly, while Peter simply nodded in agreement.

"Hey, where's the Doc?" asked Cash.

"Sorry, he's busy," answered Greta. "If there's people to take care of, the Doc won't leave them. He's like that."

"Cool, I'll see him when he's free," said Cash. "Right, now that we've got the pleasantries out of the way, let's discuss how we're going to keep our people safe," Cash said, his tone growing serious as he looked around at the faces of his advisors. "The Integration is coming, whether we like it or not. And we have a shithouse full of stuff to do if we want any chance of surviving."

"Your determination is commendable, Lord Appalachia," Greta observed, her expression unreadable.

"Damn right it is," Cash replied, his eyes flashing with resolve. "Now let's get to work. Alright, Gunny," Cash continued, grinning as he looked over at the security advisor. "I know you Marines think you're hot shit, but let's see if you can handle all the crap I'm gonna throw your way."

"Ha!" Gunny barked out a laugh. "You Army Rangers always talk a big game, but when it comes to getting the job done, I'd trust a jarhead over a snake eater any day."

"Ouch," Cash mockingly clutched at his chest with his cybernetic hand, feigning injury. "That one stung, Gunny. "But enough banter – let's get down to business, shall we? Tom, I want you to oversee city logistics, power, and accommodation. We need to make sure everything runs smoothly for our people."

"Understood, Lord Appalachia," Tom replied, jotting down notes.

"Peter," Greta interjected, "you have a keen eye for commerce. I propose you start and run a merchant's guild of some sort, also take a look at instituting some type of taxation system. Not that we'll need it now, but for the future. Just something to start thinking about."

"An excellent suggestion, Senior Advisor," Cash agreed. "Peter, do you accept the responsibility?"

"Of course, Lord Appalachia," Peter said, bowing his head slightly.

"Good, I also want you to take control of the System Shop. Allocate times, keep a check on what people are looking for, keep a tight rein on it all." He then turned his attention back to Gunny. "And Gunny, I have a special task for you. I want you to form a City Watch to patrol the walls and keep the peace in Tomahawk. Our people need to feel safe and secure, both from outside threats and within."

"Consider it done," Gunny replied, his voice firm and resolute.

"Additionally, I'd like you to look into starting an Adventurers Guild. We need a group of skilled individuals who can not only protect the town but gather resources and potentially form the core of a small standing army."

"An Adventurers Guild?" Gunny looked thoughtful for a moment. Cash readied himself to speak again, but before he did, Gunny interjected.

"Lord Appalachia," Gunny began, clearing his throat as he folded his arms across his chest, "I appreciate the trust you've placed in me, but I have to be honest: I'm not the right person to head an Adventurers Guild."

Cash raised an eyebrow, intrigued by Gunny's hesitation. The flickering light of the grand hall's braziers cast shadows that played across Gunny's weathered face, highlighting the lines etched by years of hard living and combat.

"Really?" Cash asked, a hint of amusement in

his voice. "And why's that, Gunny? You think a bunch of Rangers could handle it better than a Marine?"

"Ha!" Gunny barked a laugh, shaking his head. "Rangers can kiss my ass. No, Lord Appalachia, it's not about that. See, an Adventurers Guild is a different beast altogether. They're more... independent. Combining them with the army would be like trying to mix oil and water."

"Alright, then," Cash mused, stroking the stubble on his chin with one of his cybernetic fingers. "What do you suggest?"

"Keep the army and the Adventurers Guild separate," Gunny said decisively. "If we want a proper guild, we'll need someone who understands their unique dynamics and can manage those free-spirited bastards without stifling their creativity."

"Someone like who?" Cash pressed, genuinely curious.

"Garth Sawyer," Gunny replied without missing a beat. "Retired Chief Warrant Officer. He's got the experience, the connections, and most importantly, the patience for this shitstorm. Trust me, if anyone can wrangle a gaggle of adventurers into a well-oiled machine, it's him."

Cash considered Gunny's words, weighing the options. He knew that Gunny's judgment was solid, and his understanding of people's strengths and weaknesses was uncanny. As he looked around at his advisors, each one competent and dedicated in their own ways, Cash couldn't help but feel a swell of pride.

"Alright," Cash agreed, nodding firmly. "We'll keep the army separate from the Adventurers Guild. Have Sawyer brought in. If you vouch for him, Gunny, that's good enough for me."

"Thank you, Lord Appalachia," Gunny said, visibly relieved. "I promise, you won't regret it."

"Damn well better not," Cash muttered, only half-joking as he allowed himself a small smile. Tomahawk was depending on them, and with the Integration less than five months away, there was no room for error. "Well that's pretty much it," said Cash. "Short and sweet. Off you go, let's get stuff done. Gunny, hang fire for a few minutes."

The advisors filed out of the grand hall, leaving Cash and Gunny in the dimly lit room. The mana powered lighting flickered, casting eerie shadows on the ancient stone walls. Cash leaned against the cold stone table, his cybernetic limbs whirring softly with each subtle movement.

"Alright, let's talk more about this Garth Sawyer," Cash said, his gruff voice echoing off the high arched ceiling. "If he's going to be running this Adventurers Guild, I want to know every little goddamn detail about him."

"Figured you might." Gunny smirked, crossing his arms. "Garth served with me for a few years before retiring. He's got a knack for handling difficult personalities and keeping them in line without crushing their spirits. He's seen some shit, just like us, but he's still got a sense of humor about it all."

"Great, another joker," Cash muttered, rolling his eyes. "But can he fight? Can he lead?"

"Damn right he can," Gunny assured him. "He may be retired, but the man's still got some fight in him. And his leadership? Top-fucking-notch. People respect him, even if they don't always like what he has to say."

Cash narrowed his eyes, pondering Gunny's words. "You're sure about this guy? I mean, I trust your judgment, but this is a big deal. We can't afford to put someone in charge who's gonna fuck it all up."

"Trust me, Cash, I wouldn't suggest him if I wasn't confident in his abilities," Gunny replied, meeting Cash's steely gaze. "I know damn well how important this is."

"Alright then," Cash sighed, rubbing his chin thoughtfully. "What kind of changes do you think he'll make to the guild? I want this place to be a force to be reckoned with, not some damn social club for adventurers."

"Garth's got the same mindset, don't worry," Gunny reassured him. "He'll whip them into shape, make sure they're properly trained and equipped. And he'll create incentives for them to work together, instead of just going off on their own and getting themselves killed."

"Fine, we'll give him a shot," Cash agreed, his decision made. "But I reserve the right to kick his ass if it all goes sideways."

"Fair enough," Gunny laughed, before growing serious again. "Just remember, though, leading an Adventurers Guild isn't like leading an army. You've got to let them have a bit more freedom, or you'll lose them."

"Understood," Cash grumbled. "Truth be told, Gunny. I don't want any of this shit."

"Well I wouldn't let the people know that, Lord Appalachia." Gunny's eyes twinkled with amusement, but his tone held genuine respect. "After all, it wouldn't do much good for morale if everyone reckoned you might just up and leave at any given moment."

"Alright, Gunny," Cash said thoughtfully. "I'll bear that in mind. Now go tell Garth he just stepped up to the plate."

"Roger that, Lord Appalachia" Gunny replied with a salute, smirking as he turned on his heel and strode from the room.

CHAPTER 4

Cash Stone and Garth Sawyer sat at the huge table in Cash's grand hall.

Garth, a former Warrant Officer in the United States Army, was pretty much what Cash had expected, six feet, rangy, cropped gray hair with a neatly trimmed beard and moustache. Dark brown eyes, a weathered face and the look of a man who didn't take crap from anyone.

The ex-soldier leaned forward, his windswept face etched with determination. "Gunny tells me you want me to start and run an Adventurers Guild here in Tomahawk."

Cash nodded, his steely gaze meeting Garth's. "You're right, Garth. We can't face what's coming alone. With the System Integration closing in, we need skilled adventurers to protect our people and explore the treacherous unknown. And for that, we need a guild, a place where warriors, mages, and explorers can gather and share their experiences. But before we can build the Guildhall, we need to discuss the specifics."

Garth scratched his grizzled beard, contemplating the best course of action. "Location is key. I suggest we construct the Guildhall near the town square, right at the heart of Tomahawk. It'll be a beacon, drawing aspiring adventurers from far and wide."

Cash chuckled. "I like the way you think," he said. "Looking to the future. Nice. And you're right, a central location will make it convenient for our members and establish the Guild as a symbol of our community's strength. We'll build it strong, a testament to our resolve."

Garth's eyes sparkled with excitement. "We want it to be functional, welcoming, and to inspire awe."

Cash grinned, his fingers drumming on the tabletop. "Look, the System doesn't give me a lot of leeway," he explained. "I pretty much select Guildhall on my HUD, then it gives me a choice of levels. I'll just go for the highest I reckon we can afford without spending too many System Points. But rest assured, there'll be accommodation, offices, an armory, reception areas and a training arena at very least."

Garth nodded in excitement. "Fantastic. Now, my Lord, let's discuss the most critical aspect—the adventurers themselves. We must be selective, choosing quality over quantity. Each member must be capable and dedicated."

Cash leaned back, considering Garth's words. "You're right, Garth. We can't afford to have adventurers who lack commitment or skill. I assume you will personally interview each candidate and ensure they possess the necessary abilities to face the challenges that lie ahead."

Garth's eyes gleamed with hope. "That's not all, my lord. Our people are poor, struggling to make ends meet. I know we have a System shop now, but with so few credits available, the new adventurers won't be able to equip themselves. Will you be able to help with equipment, spells, and skills? It'll give them a fighting chance."

Cash nodded. "Of course, Garth. We can't send them into the unknown ill-prepared..." before Cash could finish his train of thought he shook his head. "Goddammit," he exclaimed. "I've been a complete idiot. Here I am committing myself to buying stuff and I have no idea if I can even afford it. Higgins," he called out. "Where the fuck are you?"

The air next to Cash shimmered and his holographic AI, Higgins appeared. Dressed in his customary black dinner suit, and white gloves. For some reason, this time he was wearing a monocle, even though he obviously did not need one.

"Hey, Higgy-baby, why didn't you remind me about the System Shop? I haven't visited it yet to see what loot I've amassed," Cash berated, his frustration evident.

Higgins's tone carried a hint of exasperation. "Sir, I did inform you multiple times. However, you were too preoccupied with your own self-pity and rudeness towards others to pay heed. Perhaps it slipped your mind amidst your childish self-indulgence."

Cash scowled, realizing the truth in Higgins's words. "Fine, fine. I admit, I've been acting like a spoiled teenager. But no more. I'll visit the System Shop immediately to assess the value of our loot and equip our people properly."

Garth Sawyer, who had been listening intently, struggled to contain a chuckle at Cash's chagrin. He coughed to cover his amusement and interjected, "My lord, it seems you have some matters to attend to. I'll leave you to it. Rest assured, I'll begin recruiting adventurers right away."

Cash nodded, appreciating Garth's dedication. "Thank you, Garth. We need capable and dedicated adventurers by our side. Let's meet again soon to discuss their progress."

As Garth took his leave, Cash walked to the balcony so he had a view of the city. Then he activated his HUD, summoning the holographic interface that allowed him to shape the world within the System. With a determined expression, he scanned through his options and chose a level 3 Adventurers Hall.

The hall materialized before him, situated within the protective walls of Tomahawk. It stood tall and imposing, a testament to the strength and unity of their community.

With a satisfied smile, Cash completed the

creation process, admiring his handiwork. The Adventurers Hall stood as a physical embodiment of his vision—a place where heroes would rise, challenges would be conquered, and the spirit of camaraderie would flourish.

As the hum of excitement coursed through his veins, Cash couldn't help but feel a renewed sense of purpose. He was no longer just a former army Ranger, crippled and scarred. He had become Lord Appalachia, a leader striving to protect his people and shape their destiny in this unforgiving new world. And for the first time, it didn't seem to suck as much as it usually did.

With a renewed sense of purpose, Cash Stone strode out of his Lord's dwelling, ready to visit the System Shop and unravel the mysteries of his loot.

As he made his way through the streets of Tomahawk, accompanied by the ever-present Higgins, he couldn't help but notice the newfound respect in the townsfolk's eyes. They greeted him with nods and smiles, their admiration evident. Cash reciprocated the gestures, determined to be more approachable, even if he still felt uncomfortable in such interactions.

Before reaching the System Shop, a soft chime resonated in Cash's ears, alerting him to a message from the System. His HUD flickered to life, displaying the notification that he had been awarded an additional Charisma point. The words seemed to taunt him, fueling his irritation.

"Another point to Charisma," Cash muttered,

his voice tinged with annoyance. "Damn it all. As if I need more of that meaningless stat. If I gain any more Charisma points, I'll be as lovable as fucking Santa Claus."

Higgins, always quick to offer a wry remark, couldn't help but chuckle. "Oh, I wouldn't worry too much, sir. Even with the extra point, you're still below the average person's Charisma stat of 10. You're far from being a paragon of charm. No need to fret about becoming too likable."

Cash scowled, his frustration evident. "Are you suggesting that I'm an asshole, Higgins?"

Higgins shook his head, a small smile playing at his lips. "Oh, perish the thought, sir. I would never say such a thing, at least not aloud. But let's just say your charm lies in other areas."

They shared a hearty laugh, the tension easing. It was moments like these that reminded Cash of the unlikely bond he had formed with his AI companion. Higgins had become more than just an assistant—he was a confidant and a friend.

The System Shop stood before Cash and Higgins, a small and unassuming structure that belied the vast potential within its walls. As the duo approached, the large sliding door glided open, revealing the enigmatic interior. Stepping inside, Cash marveled at the stark contrast between the modest exterior and the expansive space that greeted him.

The shop's interior seemed to defy the laws of space, stretching out far beyond what its physical dimensions should allow. A long, polished steel counter dominated the area, manned by six humanoid robots, their mechanical eyes scanning the room. One of the robots, its metallic voice resonating, inquired, "Can I assist you today?"

With a determined expression, Cash carefully unloaded his hard-earned loot onto the counter, driven by his burning desire to ascertain its true value and equip his people for the imminent challenges ahead.

"Woah, Higgins," exclaimed Cash. "I had no idea I had accumulated so much of this crap."

"You have killed many, many mobs, sir," said Higgins. "Not to mention a rather substantial number of Boss's as well. Sir, if I may, I suggest that I take care of the negotiations vis-à-vis the sale of said loot, while you take a chance to peruse the myriad of items available in the Shop."

"Cool, go for it," agreed Cash. "Oh, how do I check the inventory out?"

One of the robots pointed to a small circle of light. "One merely stands in that," it instructed. "The mana circle will allow your HUD access to the Shops stock and pricing."

"Thanks, metal dude," said Cash as he did as instructed and began checking out the Shops wares.

After a thorough evaluation and almost half an hour of haggling, Higgins turned to Cash, a satisfied gleam in his digital eyes. "We've managed to sell the loot for an impressive sum of 127,692 credits," Higgins announced, relaying the news of their successful negotiation. "That is enough wealth to equip a hundred adventurers with mid-range armor and weapons and even a few low-level spells, as well as invest in tools for the Crafting Hall and seeds for the farms."

Cash couldn't contain his elation, a triumphant grin spreading across his face. The weight of responsibility lifted momentarily as he imagined the prospect of his people armed and ready, their abilities enhanced by the fruits of their labor. "Well done, Higgins!" Cash exclaimed, his voice filled with genuine pride. "This is a significantly less sucky outcome than I expected. But before I buy anything, first I reckon I need to have a chat to all my advisors and make a shopping list. Hoorah! Rangers lead the way."

CHAPTER 5

Garth Sawyer, the new leader of the Tomahawk Adventurers Guild surveyed the room of new recruits. He had been surprised at the high turnout of volunteers who had pitched up, eager to join the guild and become an adventurer. Almost seventy people. But after he had interviewed them and removed the chaff from the wheat, he was left with twenty-seven souls. He was under no illusions that this number would decrease again once the training started. Not everyone was cut out to be an adventurer, no matter what they thought.

"Listen up, you goggle-faced newbies!" his voice boomed through the training hall, instantly capturing the attention of the eager adventurers-in-training. They gathered around, their eyes shining with anticipation, ready to embark on a thrilling journey of discovery within the expansive realm of this fucked up RPG world.

"Today, I shall unravel the mysteries of the

essential roles that define our world," the Guild Master declared with authority. "Each of you shall find your place as a Tank, Melee Fighter, Ranged Attacker, Rogue, or Healer!"

The recruits leaned in, their hearts pounding with excitement, eager to absorb every word that would shape their destiny.

"First, let us behold the awe-inspiring might of the Tank!" the Guild Master's voice resounded through the guild hall, commanding the attention of every aspiring adventurer. Their gaze fixated upon a three-dimensional holographic projection, depicting a towering figure adorned in armor that seemed forged from the very essence of resilience. Every surface of the armor gleamed with an ethereal luminescence, casting a radiant glow that spoke of impregnability.

"They are the indomitable guardians, stalwart and unyielding in the face of danger," the Guild Master declared, his voice infused with reverence. "Behold their colossal strength, honed through countless battles, and witness their impenetrable defense, crafted by the finest blacksmiths and enchanted by the most skilled sorcerers. In the chaotic fray of combat, they stand as the beacon of protection, drawing the ire of enemies like a magnet, shielding our comrades from harm."

Next, the Guild Master's hand swept toward a holographic projection, conjuring the image of a nimble warrior radiating an aura of controlled aggression. The glimmering blade clasped in their hand seemed to thirst for battle, its edges honed to a razor-sharp perfection. "Behold the Melee Fighter! Masters of close-quarters combat, their prowess with weapons transcends the ordinary, transforming each strike into a symphony of lethal precision. Whether wielding a sword, ax, or spear, their chosen instrument becomes an extension of their very being.

"Speed and agility are the essence of the Melee Fighter," the Guild Master's voice reverberated with reverence. "They possess an uncanny swiftness that allows them to close the distance with unparalleled rapidity, catching foes off guard and leaving them defenseless in the face of their onslaught. Their lightning-fast strikes unleash a maelstrom of devastation, cleaving through adversaries with unyielding ferocity.

"Their weapons are their companions. Whether it be a sword, an ax, or a spear that extends their reach, each choice is a reflection of their preferred style. The sword grants versatility, allowing for quick strikes and nimble parries. The ax embodies raw power, its mighty swings cleaving through armor and bone alike. And the spear, a weapon of reach, grants them the advantage of distance while maintaining lethal precision."

"Now, let your eyes be captivated by the ethereal prowess of the Ranged Attacker," said Garth, overplaying his role of Guild Commander slightly. But what the hell, he thought, he was enjoying himself. His voice resounded with a sense of wonder, punctuated by a grandiose gesture. "Armed with a variety of deadly implements such as bows, crossbows, or even ranged spells, they embody the very essence of strategic devastation. From a distance, they rain down a storm of projectiles upon their hapless foes, each shot guided by unerring accuracy and infused with unparalleled cunning!"

"Yet, it is not merely their skill with the bow or crossbow that sets them apart," the Guild Master's voice continued, a hint of mystery lingering in their words. "In the realm of arcane arts, the Ranged Attacker harnesses the raw power of mana to wield enchanted projectiles. From bolts of crackling lightning to orbs of searing flame."

The recruits gasped, their minds ignited with visions of becoming skilled archers or spellcasters, their arrows and spells bringing down enemies with deadly precision from a distance.

Garth's mischievous smile stretched wider, his eyes sparkling with a hint of intrigue, as his gaze shifted to a figure concealed within the veil of shadows. "Behold, the Rogue, a paragon of stealth and subterfuge! Swift as a phantom and elusive as a wisp of smoke, they traverse the labyrinthine depths of enemy lines, their movements a mesmerizing dance of deadly grace. With uncanny precision, they identify and exploit the most vulnerable points of their adversaries, each strike akin to the flick of a serpent's tongue, delivering devastating critical hits that leave their foes reeling in agony."

The recruits leaned forward, captivated by the enigma that shrouded the holographic representation of the Rogue. Their eyes traced the sinuous contours of the warrior's form, their steps silent and calculated, as if in harmony with the very essence of darkness itself. The Rogue's very presence seemed to defy detection, a testament to their mastery over the art of stealth.

Lastly, the Guild Master's gaze shifted, settling upon a gentle figure cloaked in flowing robes that seemed to shimmer with an ethereal glow. The air around them tingled with an aura of tranquility, casting a soothing calmness upon the room. "And last but not least, we have the Healer," the Guild Master's voice carried a reverence befitting their noble role. "These stalwarts of the sacred arts are blessed with the power of restoration, their very touch capable of mending wounds and rekindling the flickering embers of life itself. Through their mastery of divine or arcane abilities, they ensure our comrades stand unyielding, facing the tempests of adversity with renewed vigor."

The recruits' gazes fixated on the healer, their eyes widening with a newfound appreciation for the subtle strength that emanated from the figure before them. The intricate embroidery adorning the healer's robes seemed to shimmer with hues of celestial energy, symbolizing the intertwining of magic and compassion that defined their craft.

"Now, my wannabe adventurers, embrace the path that calls to your heart," the Guild Master declared. "Decide what path you would like to follow. Once you have done so, come and see me so I can tell you how fucking wrong you are. Or maybe I shall agree with you, one never knows. After that, we will start your training, equip you with armor, weapons and spells, hone your skills, and let unwavering determination flow through your veins. Together, we shall confront the challenges of this shit-eating RPG realm, and we shall emerge triumphant!"

The recruits erupted in cheers, their spirits buoyed by a sense of purpose and camaraderie. The Guild Master's eyes gleamed with pride and anticipation, for in these aspiring heroes, they saw the potential to shape destinies and etch their mark upon the new, shitty, ever-evolving tapestry of their new fucked up world.

CHAPTER 6

Cash Stone stood in the center of the Adventurers Guild, his cybernetic limbs humming as he clenched and unclenched his fists. Memories of battles fought and comrades lost lingered in his mind, reminding him that the world outside was a dangerous place. But it was also a place where they could make a difference.

"Fuck it," Cash muttered to himself. "These kids need better gear if they're going to survive out there."

"Did I hear you correctly, my Lord?" Garth, the head of the Adventurers Guild, asked as he approached. "Are you really considering spending your credits on new equipment for the guild members?"

"Yeah, I am," Cash replied, his gruff voice betraying a hint of vulnerability. "I told you before that I would take care of them. But don't go blabberin' about it, alright? I've got a reputation to maintain."

"Of course, of course," Garth agreed with a chuckle. "Your secrets are safe with me. Now, we'll need enough equipment to outfit five tanks, five

Rogues, five Melee Fighters, five Ranged Fighters, and five healers. Armor, weapons, spell scrolls... whatever they'll need to hold their own out there."

"Got it," Cash nodded, mentally tallying up the costs. He knew it would put a significant dent in his personal stash of credits, but he couldn't shake the feeling that he needed to do this - not just for the guild, but for himself as well.

"Are you sure about this?" Garth asked, concern etched on his face. "You've worked hard to earn those credits."

"Look, Garth," Cash growled, his eyes narrowing. "I ain't doin' this for shits and giggles. I'm doin' this because these guys and girls deserve a chance to fight, and I'll be damned if I let 'em go out there with piss-poor gear."

"Alright then," Garth said, clapping Cash on the shoulder. "We appreciate it, truly."

"Whatever," Cash grumbled, brushing off the gratitude. The last thing he needed was a pat on the back for being a decent human being. Without saying any more, he made his way to the shop, followed closely by Higgins and Bonny.

After a few minutes of walking, he stepped into the System shop with its stark clinical interior, long steel counter and robot assistance.

"Ah, Lord Appalachia," greeted one of the robots. "What can I help you find today?"

"Need gear," Cash grunted, his. "Actually, Higgins, you heard what Garth needs, can you take care of things? I'm gonna see if there's anything specific that I might be able to use."

"Of course, sir," confirmed Higgins as he approached the robot shop assistant and rattled off the list.

"Quite the shopping list," the robot remarked. "But I am sure we can accommodate your needs. Let us start with the armor, shall we?"

"Make it quick," Cash growled. "And don't let them upsell us on bullshit we don't need."

"Please, sir," admonished Higgins. "I assure you, I have this under control."

"And make sure the equipment can be upgraded as the users level up?" Cash added.

Higgins rolled his holographic eyes, and Cash, taking the hint, left his AI assistant to it.

While Higgins took care of the order, Cash checked out the other goods available. To be honest, he wasn't actually looking for anything specific, he was merely passing the time until Higgins and the robot had concluded the business.

Finally, Higgins made a show of clearing his throat to attract Cash's attention. "Sir, the Adventurers Guild is taken care of. Is there anything else?"

"Yep," confirmed Cash. trying to sound amicable despite his irritation. "Got some more mundane equipment that needs purchasin'. Blacksmithing forge, leatherworking station, alchemy supplies... and skill books. Lots of 'em. Also, seeds, the usual, grains, legumes, vegetables. All that boring shit for the farms. Not sure much we need, just get a few sacksful of each."

Twenty minutes later, Higgins showed Cash the bill. And to Cash's credit he didn't pass out as he transferred the credits to the shops account.

"Fuckin' bastard shopping spree," he muttered, rubbing his temples. He checked his account balance, wishing he hadn't: 9,812 credits. Just under ten grand left from what had once been a small fortune.

"Damn it all," he grumbled, "I'm practically broke. Hey, metal-man," Cash gestured to the robot. "I assume that for that price you deliver?"

"Yes, sir," affirmed the shop assistant. "In fact your AI has already told me where the goods must be sent. They will arrive within minutes."

"Great," mumbled Cash. "Now let's get the hell outa here before I get raped. Again."

***

Cash strode through the busy streets towards the Adventurers Guild, determined to stock up on supplies before venturing out into the great unknown. As he walked, his cybernetic limbs whirred softly with each step, a constant reminder of the battles he'd fought and the price he'd paid. Bonny trotted happily alongside him, her ears perked up and her tail wagging.

"Alright, girl," Cash muttered under his breath as they approached the guild's entrance. "We need to get ourselves some more loot. I was rich for a short bit, and now I'm fucking poor again. Time to get out there and start killing shit. Let's see if Sarah might be up for this little expedition."

Cash found Sarah at the Crafting Hall and after he explained his plan, she nodded.

"I may not be a seasoned fighter like you two, but I can hold my own in battle," she said. "And any opportunity to Level up is a good thing."

"Of course," Cash agreed, surprised by how pleased he was to have her join them. He had grown accustomed to facing down danger alone, but lately, he found himself not relishing the camaraderie of a fellow adventurer, but at least not hating the thought.

"First, we find ourselves some Boss mobs," Cash said, fixing Sarah and Bonny with a determined stare. "They're bound to have the best loot, obviously."

"Sounds good to me," Lady Sarah agreed, her eyes twinkling with excitement. "What about you, Higgins? Ready for some Boss hunting?"

"I live to serve, my Lady," replied Higgins dryly.

"Alright, then," Cash declared, his heart pounding with anticipation. "Let's gear up and get moving."

"Lead the way, fearless leader," Lady Sarah said, giving him an impish smile as she fell into step beside him.

"Yeah, whatever," quipped Cash. "I had better inform Greta that we'll be gone for a bit, then let's do this."

Before he set off, Cash called up his Character

CRAIG ZERF

Sheet just to reacquaint himself with his stats.

Name: Cash Stone	Class: Cyberknight Level: 26	Experience Points XP 1550000 (2000000)	Hit Points HP 525 (50) (25 per minute)	Stamina ST 525 (25 per minute)	Mana Points MP 475 (20 per minute)
Strength 21	Constitution 20	Agility 21	Dexterity 7	Mind 28	Charisma 8
System Points 152				**Credits** 0	
Weapons – Elemental Ax – Level 5 Cybernetic crossbow – Level 5					
Perks - Personal cybernetic enhancements – Level 5 Cybernetic Armor – Level 5					
Titles – Ursine Exterminator Eager Beaver Lord Appalachia Giant Killer					
Spells – Lightning Bolt – Level 5					
Companions – Bonny Stone Boss Hunter Level: 18	Hit Points HP 400 (12 per Minute)	Strength 16	Constitution 16	Agility 117	Mind 6

CHAPTER 7

The Appalachian Forest was a breathtaking sight to behold, with towering trees that stretched skyward like ancient giants. Their branches formed a thick canopy overhead, casting dappled sunlight on the dense undergrowth below. The forest floor teemed with life; insects skittered among the twisted roots while Labrador sized squirrels chased each other through the foliage and birds the size of Condors squawked raucously from the treetops. The System had accelerated all growth to the point that even the forest flowers were now as large as pre-apocalyptic trees.

"Fuck me sideways with a wire brush," Cash Stone muttered, as he hacked away at a stubborn vine blocking their path. "This place is greener than a leprechaun's asshole. One would think that massive flowers should be pretty, but they're just fucking creepy."

"Language, Cash," Sarah Connor chided him with a smirk. "Don't say Leprechaun, it's as stupid word."

"Sorry, Sarah," Cash replied, rolling his eyes but not really meaning it. "Just trying to get us through this goddamn jungle."

"Forest, actually," she corrected him, her tone playful.

"Whatever," he grumbled, swatting away a particularly aggressive mosquito that was larger than a crow.

Bonny trotted along at Cash's side, her ears perked and her keen senses alert. Her unwavering loyalty and intelligence made her an invaluable ally in these treacherous times. A soft growl rumbled deep in her throat, a warning to her master that danger might be lurking just around the bend.

"Easy, girl," Cash whispered, his hand going to the hilt of his ax. "What's got your fur all ruffled?"

"Fuck!" Cash spat out as he caught a glimpse of the ferocious pack of iron-wolves stalking towards them. Their fur was like steel chain mail, their razor-sharp claws glinted in the dappled sunlight that filtered through the dense canopy above, and their fangs were made of unforgiving metal.

"Sarah, we've got company!" he shouted, his cybernetic hand tightening around the hilt of his ax.

"Well, that's what we're here for" Sarah yelled, her eyes widening at the sight of the snarling beasts. She didn't waste any time, immediately beginning to conjure a fireball in her right hand.

"Bonny! Guard our flank!" ordered Cash as he used Identify on the pack.

Iron Wolf *- Level 25*
HP *- 250/250*
Weakness *- Lightning based attacks.*
Strength *- Crushing bite.*

The loyal Tamaskan dog bared her teeth and growled, taking up position beside her master. Her nimble legs tensed, ready to spring into action at a moment's notice.

"Alright, you metal fuckers," Cash said under his breath, bracing himself for the onslaught. "Let's dance."

As the first iron-wolf leapt towards them, its snarl sending chills down Cash's spine, he swung his ax expertly, slicing through the air with a whistling sound. The ax met the wolf's steel hide with a resounding clang, but it did little to slow the creature down. It lunged again, teeth snapping mere inches from Cash's face.

"Damn it, these things are tough!" Cash grunted, his muscles straining with each blow he landed on the wolves. Meanwhile, Sarah focused her efforts on casting fireballs at the approaching creatures. The scent of singed fur filled the air as the flames licked at the wolves' steel hides, sending some of them yelping back into the underbrush.

Cash powered up a bolt of lightning and flung it. The spell was the perfect attack to use against the iron wolves as it crackled and leaped from wolf to wolf, dealing massive amounts of damage as it did so.

Bonny darted in and out of the fray, her lithe body avoiding the slashing claws and snapping jaws of the iron-wolves. She nipped at their heels, drawing their attention away from Cash and Sarah, giving them valuable time to regroup and strategize.

"Okay, new plan," Cash panted, his breath coming in short gasps as he fended off another wolf. "My lightning works great, but it's mana heavy, Sarah, try your magma missile, see if it'll melt through their armor?"

"Sounds like a plan," she replied, gritting her teeth as she concentrated her magical energy into a single, searing point of heat. The targeted wolf yowled in pain as its metallic hide began to soften and give way under the intense heat.

"Good! Now let's finish this!" Cash bellowed, finally finding an opening in the softened metal. He swung his ax with all his might, cleaving through the weakened armor and into the flesh beneath. The iron-wolf fell, its lifeless body slumping to the forest floor. "Batter up, he swings, and it's a home run," yelled Cash.

The trio rushed towards the remaining iron-wolves with a wild ferocity, wielding their weapons and spells with reckless abandon. With every movement, they launched bolts of arcane energy and parried the wolves lunges with deft precision. The air was thick with sweat and desperation, yet they trudged forward, for they knew this was the only way to survive this seemingly never-ending battle against the unrelenting iron-wolves.

"Is that the last of them?" Cash asked, surveying the carnage around them. His ax was slick with blood, and his cybernetic limbs ached with overexertion.

"Seems like it," Sarah confirmed, her eyes scanning the treeline for any lingering threats. "But we'd better stay sharp. There's no telling what other creations await us in this shitty forest."

"Never a dull moment, huh?" Cash quipped, his grim expression belying the humor in his words.

"Welcome to the apocalypse," Sarah replied with a wry smile.

***

"I would advise sticking close to the riverbed," Higgins suggested, his synthesized voice crackling in the air. "There's a higher probability of encountering more hostile mobs there."

"Great," grumbled Cash, readjusting the grip on his ax. "More beasts that wanna rip our faces off."

"Well, sir, as lady Sarah pointed out earlier, that is why you are out here."

Before Cash could think up a snarky rejoiner, a thunderous roar echoed through the forest, sending shivers down their spines. Towering above them was a monstrous Boss mob - a colossal, mutated Horned-Bear with massive tusks protruding from its snout and spikes covering its hulking form. It roared again, saliva dripping from its gaping maw as it lunged toward them.

"Hey, its Winnie the Pooh's pissed bigger, psychotic uncle. No sweat, I eat bears for brekkie. Sort of." Cash bellowed, swinging his ax at the behemoth's legs, relying on his Ursine Exterminator title to increase his damage against the bear.

Sarah cast her Necrotic spell and it settled on the bear like a miasma, eating into its thick hide and causing it to bellow in pain.

"Bonny, go for the throat!" Cash ordered, his heart pounding as they fought for their lives.

"Actually, sir," Higgins interjected, "I would recommend targeting the exposed armpit area. My scans indicate a weak point in its hide there."

"Really? Now you tell me?" Cash huffed, but he knew better than to question Higgins' tactical analysis. He charged forward, leaping onto the bear's front leg and using his cybernetic strength to propel himself upwards, ax poised for a lethal strike.

"Cover me, Sarah!" he yelled, plunging the ax deep into the beast's armpit. The bear let out an earth-shattering roar and swiped at Cash, who narrowly avoided the massive claws.

"Got your back, buddy," Sarah shouted, unleashing a magma missile to blast the bear's face once more.

"Keep hitting that weak spot, Cash! We can do this!" she encouraged, her voice laced with determination.

"Damn straight," Cash grunted, landing another powerful blow to the vulnerable area. "Bonny, keep its attention on you!"

The loyal Tamaskan dog obeyed, nipping at the bear's legs and darting just out of reach each time it tried to retaliate.

"Sarah, Bonny, on my mark!" Cash bellowed, readying one final, desperate strike. "Now!"

As Sarah unleashed a fireball, Bonny lunged for the bear's throat, sinking her teeth into its flesh. With a primal scream, Cash drove his ax deep into the Boss mob's armpit, severing ribs and flesh and causing it to collapse in agony. He followed up with a barrage of mana bolts from his crossbow that dropped the bear's HP to zero.

"Fuck yeah!" Cash whooped, panting heavily as they stood over the fallen beast. "That's how you take down a goddamn monster."

"Teamwork," Sarah grinned, looking equal parts exhausted and exhilarated. "And one hell of a good swing."

"Thanks, both of you," Cash said, his voice thick with gratitude. "And Higgins, your advice saved our asses again."

"Of course, sir," Higgins stated dryly. "I am here to serve."

"Alright, we still got places to go and mobs to kill," Cash sighed, wiping blood from his face.

"Let's get moving."

***

The sun dipped below the horizon, casting elongated shadows across the forest floor as Cash and his team trekked deeper into the heart of the Appalachian woods. The air was thick with the scent of damp earth and decay, a potent reminder of the once-thriving ecosystem now overrun by monstrous creatures.

"Alright, listen up," Cash said, his voice low and gravelly. "We've got an ugly fucker up ahead. I've never seen one like this before, so we need to coordinate our attacks. My Identification lists it as an Armored Arachnoid-Serpent."

"Great, another new monstrosity to add to our collection," Sarah muttered, shifting her grip on her staff. "How are we doing this?"

"Bonny, I want you to flank from the left, keep it distracted," Cash instructed. "Sarah, I'll need your arcane fuckery to weaken it while I go for the kill."

"Wouldn't have it any other way," Sarah replied with a grin, as she prepared her spellwork.

"Alright, on three," Cash counted down. "One... two... three!"

They sprang into action, Bonny darting through the underbrush towards the grotesque creature that lay in wait. It was a horrifying fusion of snake and spider, its long, sinuous body covered in a chitinous exoskeleton, and its many legs clicking against the leaf-strewn ground as it lunged forward to meet them.

"Fuck me, that thing's nasty," Cash thought as he charged, ax at the ready.

Bonny nipped at the monster's legs, her lithe form evading its snapping jaws with ease. Sarah unleashed a torrent of fire, the tendrils of flame enveloping the creature and causing it to screech in pain.

"Bonny, watch out for..." Cash began, but his warning came too late. A barbed tail swiped through the air, catching Bonny in the side and sending her flying into a nearby tree trunk with a sickening thud.

"Bonny!" Cash roared, fury igniting within him as he charged the creature head-on.

"Shit, shit, shit," Sarah muttered under her breath, adrenaline coursing through her veins as she switched tactics. Pouring every ounce of energy she had into her next spell, she cried out, "Cash, duck!"

Cash instinctively dropped to the ground, narrowly avoiding the blast of arcane fire that shot from Sarah, engulfing the monster in searing flames.

"Sarah, are you alright?" Cash called out, concern etched on his face as he noticed her clutching her arm.

"Fine," she gritted out, her voice strained with pain. "Just took some backlash from that spell, suffering from some serious mana depletion. Keep going, I've got this!"

"Fuck this thing," Cash thought as he leapt to his feet, ax swinging wildly. With each blow landed, the creature shrieked and writhed in agony.

"Finish it, Cash!" Sarah yelled, her voice hoarse from exertion.

"Here's one for Bonny, you son of a bitch!" he roared, bringing his ax down with bone-crushing force, cleaving the creature's skull in two.

The monster fell limp, its remains smoking from the magic that had been used against it.

"Nice shot," Sarah wheezed, slumping against a tree. "Now let's get Bonny patched up before I pass out."

"Right." Cash nodded grimly, scooping up Bonny's limp form and cradling her gently in his arms as he activated his Healing spell. Bonny twitched as the spell took effect, and after Cash cast it the second time, she managed a weak huff. "Son of a bitch," breathed Cash in relief. "Don't do that again, you stupid mutt." He hugged his companion closely.

"Arf!"

***

As they continued through the forest, they heard the sounds of battle ringing out. Cash led his team towards the sounds, running as fast as he could.

They burst into a clearing, and in the middle

of it they saw a group of fresh-faced adventurers from the newly minted Tomahawk Adventurers Guild. The group was locked in battle with a monstrous Boss mob that resembled a giant, mutated boar with six legs and viciously sharp, bone spikes jutting from its back.

"Holy crap," Cash muttered, watching as the newbies struggled to fend off the beast's relentless attacks. "They're gonna get themselves killed. Hey, you overgrown piglet!" Cash shouted as he neared the monster. With a powerful swing, he brought his fist down hard on one of the bone spikes jutting from the creature's back.

The spike shattered under the force of his blow, the beast rearing back in pain and surprise. The shockwave rippled outwards, stunning the beast momentarily.

"Move your asses!" Cash yelled at the newbies, who seemed frozen in shock at his sudden intervention.

The group's leader, snapped out of his stupor and began barking orders at his team, coordinating their attacks once more.

"Keep up the pressure!" Cash shouted, dodging a swipe from the boar's massive claws. He could feel sweat trickling down the small of his back, mixing with the blood from his own wounds – but goddamnit, they were going to win this fucking battle.

"Sarah, now!" he yelled, and a burst of fire shot past him, striking the monster in its exposed flank. It roared in pain, giving Cash the opening he needed.

"Take this, you piece of shit!" Cash snarled, leaping into the air and driving his ax deep into the creature's skull with all the strength he could muster. The beast collapsed with an earth-shaking thud, dead at last.

"Fuck yeah!" Sarah cheered, appearing at Cash's side as the adrenaline began to fade. "That was one hell of a fight!"

Cash turned to face the group of newbies. "Hi," he said. "I'm Cash."

There was as general mumble and one of them stepped forward. "We know who you are, my lord," he said. "And thank you for pulling our asses out of the fire. Please allow me to introduce my team"

There were five of them: their leader, a charismatic rogue by the name of Darius who was currently talking to Cash. A massive, red-headed Tank named Flynn; an archer called Lyra; a melee fighter called Titch; and a quiet Healer monk named Sasha.

Cash acknowledged each of them as they were introduced. Then he turned back to Darius. "Next time you take on a mob," Cash told him, clapping him on the back, "maybe make sure you don't pick something twenty levels above you, alright? Trust me, there is no shame in running away."

"Unless of course you do it while screaming like a baby and pissing your pants," added Sarah with a grin.

"Thanks for the advice," Darius replied, rolling his eyes but smiling all the same. "And thanks again for saving our asses."

"Anytime, kid." Cash smirked. "Now why don't we all go back to Tomahawk, I got some loot to flog."

CHAPTER 8

With his share of the loot in his inventory, Cash led the newbie Adventurers together with Sarah, Bonny, and Higgins back to the city of Tomahawk. The towering walls welcomed them with a sense of familiarity and security, reminding them of their accomplishments and the thriving community they had built.

As they entered the city gates, the bustling marketplace greeted them with a chorus of merchants' calls and the aroma of exotic spices. Cash made his way to the System Shop, eager to exchange his spoils for credits. As usual, Higgins took care of the negotiations while Cash stood aside and chatted to Sarah.

"Ah, sir, you've outdone yourself this time," Higgins exclaimed, a hint of awe in his voice. "In such a short time you have managed to make yourself 75,000 credits."

Cash nodded, accepting the payment with a sense of satisfaction. The credits would prove invaluable for the growth and prosperity of

Tomahawk.

However, before delving into his own plans, Cash understood the importance of entrusting some of the funds to his trusted advisor.

He sought out Greta, his senior advisor, the shrewd and kick ass woman whose counsel he valued deeply. As he saw her, he called up her HUD and transferred 50,000 credits over to her. Greta's eyebrows rose in surprise as he did so.

"Wow, my lord," she commented. "That's a shithouse full of credits. What's it for? Can I buy myself a pony?"

Cash chuckled. "Sure, whatever. But seriously, Greta, I trust your judgment. You just do whatever you think is in the best interests of Tomahawk."

Greta smiled. "Thanks, boss."

As Cash made his way to the Crafting Hall, he felt a thrill of anticipation. The rich scent of fire hung heavy in the air; the clang and spark of metal filled the space with life; and the artisan craftsmen and women worked diligently at their posts. When the burly blacksmith saw him, his eyes widened in surprise and awe as he dropped his hammer and hastily wiped sweat from his brow.

"Lord Cash!" he exclaimed, bowing deeply before taking off his soot-stained apron. "You honor us with your presence. We owe you our success."

Cash flashed a smile and nodded to the blacksmith, admiring the tools and equipment that had been honed to perfection under his brief tenure. He exchanged pleasantries with the craftsman, talking about their recent projects and ideas for the Crafting Hall's future. As he left, Cash felt an immense sense of pride and accomplishment swell within him from the respect shown to him by the blacksmith and other crafters.

Having ensured the welfare of the artisans, Cash proceeded to the Adventurers Guild, a bustling hub of aspiring heroes seeking fame and fortune. Garth, the ex-soldier and Warrant Officer, stood at the helm, overseeing the guild's operations.

"Lord Cash, it's good to see you," Garth greeted with a nod. "The guild is flourishing. We're training the new recruits, and some of them have already gone on their first adventures. Your presence here reminds them of the path they've chosen."

"Yeah," said Cash. "I know. I came across a team of newbies, led by a rogue, name of Darius. Honestly, they were all about to become dead. Luckily, I helped them out and stopped that from happening."

Garth scowled. "I see, Darius hasn't reported back yet."

"Well he's in the city. I know because I escorted them back."

"I'll see he gets a dressing down," said Garth. "He's a good man, but tends to rush in without thinking."

"Obviously, just remind the fucker that a team of dead adventurers is no good to us."

"Sure thing, my lord."

Cash surveyed the rest of the guild hall, observing the new adventurers in training, honing their skills and forging friendships. He exchanged a few pleasantries with Garth, discussing their shared passion for exploration and the challenges they had encountered on their respective journeys.

With the Adventurers Guild thriving, Cash's attention turned to another vital aspect of Tomahawk's development—the newly formed Peacekeepers force. Gunny, a former Marine, led this disciplined unit, ensuring the safety and order of the city.

Gunny's weathered face lit up with a smile as Cash entered the barracks. "Lord Cash, what brings you here today?" he inquired, his military demeanor softened by respect for the man before him.

Cash and Gunny engaged in a conversation about the Peacekeepers' progress and their ongoing training. They discussed the need for additional resources, weapons, and armor to fortify their ranks. Cash assured Gunny that Greta held the authority to provide the necessary funds, emphasizing the importance of their continued partnership and the well-being of Tomahawk.

With his duties fulfilled, Cash retreated to his Lord's dwelling, a place of respite and reflection. As he reclined in his chair, contemplating the next stage of his plans, a sense of satisfaction washed over him. Tomahawk flourished under his leadership, and its future held limitless possibilities.

With renewed determination, he prepared to embark on the next chapter of his journey, knowing that every decision would shape the destiny of his RPG realm.

It was time to step things up a notch or two. He needed to get out there and start getting proactive. Time to grow his realm and search for more survivors. Even though he really did not want to take on more responsibility, Cash knew he had to. Because if he didn't then who would.

He leaned over and scratched Bonny's ears.

"Hey girl," he said. "I think it's time we got out there and found some more survivors to bring in to the fold. You agree?"

"Arf!"

CHAPTER 9

Cash frowned. This was the third town he had come across that had been almost totally destroyed. No survivors. Not even a trace.

"Holy crap," he swore. "I really expected to find some living human beings by now. What the hell happened here? Three towns. And the last one must have had a few thousand people before the douchebag apocalypse. How come there ain't no survivors?"

Higgins shrugged his holographic shoulders and adjusted his monocle. A recent affectation that he was determined to keep, no matter how much Cash ragged on him about it. "The whole of the Appalachian region is swimming in excess mana," he said. "As a result, the mobs here are extremely high levels. However, there is something wrong. Even with this level of ambient mana, there shouldn't be such wholesale destruction and death."

"So what gives?" asked Cash.

Higgins scowled. "I don't want to talk out of turn, sir. And I would merely be speculating at any rate."

"Speculate away, Higgins," urged Cash. "Spit it out."

"It seems to me that the Overlords may have taken a definite interest in this area. And specifically, in you, sir."

"Why?"

"Most likely they find you to be entertaining, sir. After all, as I have said before, the main reason the Overlords institute these RPG apocalypses is for their own amusement."

"I thought you said they did it to protect us from ourselves, or some such stupid shit."

"That is part of the reason, sir," admitted Higgins. "But recently, in the last few hundred years or so, they have definitely become more hedonistic and less altruistic."

"So, more douche-baggy than ever."

"Precisely, sir. As I believe you said before, they have become a proper bouquet of dicks."

Cash shook his head. On reflection, maybe he should have let Sarah accompany him on this mission. But he really did want a bit of alone time. Well, alone with Bonny and Higgins. But they didn't really count. He just wanted to spend a bit of time without feeling responsible for another human being. Okay, ostensibly he knew he was at some stage going to find some survivors, then obviously he would be with people again. And most likely he would be responsible for their safety. Or at least he would feel like he was.

But there was no denying that the last couple of days had been tough. To keep coming across these towns with no survivors was becoming more than a little depressing. On the plus side, he had fought a number of fairly high-level mobs, plus two Boss mobs. And as a result, he had leveled up to 27 and had garnered quite a bit of loot.

"Come on, Higgins," Cash said wearily. "Let's keep going. If memory serves, there's quite a large town a few more miles from here. Might as well take a look for it. If we push hard, should make it there before sundown. Unless we come across a bunch of mobs."

Higgins nodded, his face a mask of stoicism. Bonny whined in agreement as if she could sense the fatigue that washed over her owner's body. Cash patted her head affectionately before standing up and shouldering his ax. He took one long look at the empty town they were leaving behind and sighed.

As much as he hated to admit it, he was actually getting used to these deserted ghost towns with their remnants of destruction and death scattered about like forgotten toys. The RPG Overlords had fucked humanity good and proper. Cash sighed again. Nothing he could do except push on.

They had been traveling for half an hour when they heard guttural moans coming from ahead;

groaning sounds that made shivers run down their spines even before they could see anything. Cash's heart sank as he realized they had stumbled upon another horde of undead. He drew his ax and squinted into the distance, trying to make out how many there were.

"Shit," he muttered under his breath as Bonny growled beside him. "I hate these SOB's, they're too human. I feel like a mass murderer every time I fight them."

"As I have explained previously, sir," stated Higgins. "These are system generated creatures. They are not zombies, or any manner of former human beings who have been revived via arcane magic. I do realize they still look…human, I suppose. But rest assured, they are not."

"Yeah whatever," grunted Cash. The undead creatures had already spotted them and began stumbling toward them with surprising speed given their decayed state. Cash counted at least twenty in this group alone, with more undoubtedly lurking nearby.

He quickly used Identify and noted that they were a higher level than any of the shamblers he had fought before. There levels varied between 15 and 25. This wasn't going to be a walk in the park.

Bonny attacked first, and Cash followed up with his ax. But despite their efforts, the swarm continued forward relentlessly until Cash found himself backpedaling furiously while hacking at arms and legs that reached for him from all sides.

As he fought, Cash couldn't help but notice how unnervingly coordinated the undead were. Their movements weren't stiff or clumsy like zombies from old horror movies; they moved with a frightening sense of purpose.

Suddenly, one of the undead stumbled forward and landed at Cash's feet. He stepped back instinctively, ready to deliver a killing blow - but something made him pause.

The creature before him was different from any zombie he had seen before. It looked...alive? The skin wasn't gray and rotting like the others; it was pale and smooth as if freshly washed. Its eyes were sunken in deep sockets, yet still glinted with intelligence.

For a moment time seemed to stop as Cash stared down at this strange being that defied all logic. But then it lunged for his throat with surprising speed and strength.

Adrenaline surged through Cash's veins as he dodged its attack by mere inches. This thing wasn't just cognizant - it was making planned decisions. This was seriously fucking dangerous! And it was a new level of threat.

He swung his ax at it with all his might, but the creature was too quick and agile. It dodged his attack easily and countered with a swift kick to Cash's gut.

As he stumbled back, gasping for breath, Bonny leaped forward and ripped out a huge portion of the creature's neck. But instead of falling, its eyes flashed red as if in anger before it jerked upright again.

Cash couldn't believe what he was seeing.

"Holy crap, Higgins," yelled Cash. "This thing refuses to die."

"Well, technically, sir, it is already dead. But I understand your frustration. May I ask why you are insisting on only using your ax?"

Cash snorted. "Because," he grunted as he wound up a lightning spell and unleased it point blank into the top of the undead monster's head. There was a bright blue flash, followed by the nauseating stench of burning rotten flesh and the monsters head literally exploded, showering Cash and Bonny with foul globs of putrid flesh.

Bonny looked at Cash with a look of disgust, as if to say – Seriously? Opposing thumbs and an IQ over 120 and still you cover us in decomposing meat.

Cash rolled his eyes at Bonny's disapproving expression. "Hey, I didn't ask for the explosion," he muttered, wiping off some of the gore from his face with a disgusted grunt.

Bonny simply shook her head and made a sound that sounded suspiciously like a sigh before turning to survey their surroundings cautiously.

Cash changed his battle tactic, stashing his ax in his Inventory and loading up his crossbow. He unleashed a combination of lightning and mana bolts, tearing the remaining undead mobs to shreds with mere minutes. When the last one sank to the forest floor, Cash quickly looted them and then called Bonny to follow him.

"Okay, Higgins," he said. "Let's keep going."

Although the battle with the undead had slowed them down, the team still made good enough time to get close enough to the town Cash was searching for before the sun went down. Unlike the ghost towns he had come across earlier, this one showed obvious signs of life. But before he rushed in, Cash decided to do a thorough recon of the area first.

Cash surveyed the outskirts of the town with a cautious eye, his senses heightened by the presence of survivors. The once vibrant streets were now eerily empty, save for the occasional flicker of movement from the huddled figures inside the town hall. The town itself had seen better days, its buildings worn and weathered by the RPG accelerated passage of time and neglect.

The survivors had attempted to create a wall of sorts, piles of now defunct vehicles, furniture and rubble. It wasn't totally useless, but it was a far cry from the awesome stone edifice that protected Tomahawk, or even the much smaller wall around Peach Hamlet. Cash slipped through easily.

Bonny padded silently at Cash's side, her nose twitching as she sniffed the air, catching traces of desperation and fear.

As they cautiously made their way through the dilapidated buildings, they encountered the remnants of a once-bustling marketplace. Empty stalls, broken crates, and discarded belongings were scattered about, testament to the chaos that had befallen the town. The signs of struggle were evident, as if the survivors had fought tooth and nail to protect what little they had left.

Drawing closer to the town hall, the focal point of the survivors' sanctuary, Cash's heart sank. The building stood before him, its grandeur reduced to a weary facade. Guards, armed with makeshift weapons, patrolled its perimeter with weary eyes and slumped shoulders. Their determination was evident, but their lack of resources and equipment was disheartening.

He crept closer and peered through one of the windows to be met with a scene of somber desolation. The survivors, approximately fifty in number, huddled together, their expressions worn and their bodies weakened by hardship. The air inside the hall was thick with a sense of despair, mingled with the unmistakable stench of unsanitary conditions.

Cash's gaze swept over the room, his eyes taking in the sight of pale faces and sunken eyes. Some were visibly ill, their frail forms trembling with each labored breath. It was clear that these survivors had endured unimaginable hardships, their resilience tested to its limits.

Cash felt a pang of sympathy for the survivors. He had seen firsthand what life was like outside of these walls, and it wasn't much better than what they were facing now. With supplies dwindling

and no end to the apocalypse in sight, he knew that their chances were slim at best.

As Bonny nuzzled his hand reassuringly, Cash made up his mind. These people needed help, and he was going to provide it.

He quietly approached one of the guards patrolling outside the town hall with a kind smile on his face.

"Higgins, make yourself scarce," he whispered. "I'll introduce you later."

Higgins faded into invisibility as asked.

Cash cleared his throat to attract the guard's attention, and the young man got such a shock he almost dropped his spear.

"Wait, I mean halt," he squeaked, his voice jumping an octave as his nerves cramped his vocal cords.

Cash held his hands up to show he was unarmed. "Hey, relax," he said, his voice soft and low. "I'm a friend. Or at least I want to be. This here is Bonny, my dog. Look, we're here to help. You reckon you could call someone else and we could get to having a chat?"

"Who are you? How did you get past the walls?"

Cash chuckled. "Would we call that pile of junk a wall?" Now that he was closer to the guard, Cash could tell how young he actually was. He couldn't be more than sixteen or seventeen. Although he was so undernourished, he might actually be a bit older. "Listen, son, just go and call someone else.

Whoever's in charge. Okay, I promise I'll just stand here."

Before the teenager could respond, two men came running up, like the teenager they were both carrying spears.

"Don't move," yelled the one man. "Get on your knees. Do it now."

Cash laughed out loud and even Bonny seemed to snicker. "Yeah, not gonna happen," he said. "But I tell you what, if you don't stop pointing those sticks at me, I'll shove them so far up your ass they'll come out the top of your head."

"You dare threaten us?"

Cash sighed. "Look, guys, play nice okay. I'm here to make friends and help, so ditch the attitude before I get pissed."

"There are three of us," said the guard. At that moment, another two pitched up. "And now there's five," he continued, stating the obvious.

"Fine," said Cash. "So you're outnumbered one-to-five. Look buddy, who is in charge here."

"Might be me," answered the guard.

"Sure, in your dreams. Go get the boss. Now."

Bonny, sending Cash's frustration growled and raised her hackles. All five of the guards stepped back.

"Okay, I'll go fetch Tom," said the guard who had been talking to Cash. "But not because you told me to. I'm doing it because I want to."

Cash shook his head. "Whatever makes you feel better about yourself," he said.

As the guard left to fetch the town's leader, Cash leaned against a nearby wall, his eyes scanning the area for any potential threats. Bonny stood by his side, her sharp senses alert and ready for action.

After a few minutes, the guard returned with a middle-aged man in tow. He had a grizzled beard and wore a tattered suit that was once probably expensive. His eyes glinted with suspicion as he examined Cash from head to toe.

"Who are you and what is your business here?" he asked, his voice laced with authority.

Cash straightened up, his body tense but composed. "My name is Cash," he said. "I'm just passing through these parts. I came across your town and saw that you were in need of help."

The man raised an eyebrow. "And why should I trust you? For all I know, you could be here to take advantage of us."

Cash shook his head. "I can understand your skepticism," he said. "But I assure you, I'm here to offer help. Now, I'm not gonna beg you to accept it, but it looks to me like you dudes could use all the help you can get. I see the guards are all level 1, you're the leaders and you're only level 3. So pretty much babes in the wood and all that."

"How can you tell our levels?" asked Tom with a frown.

"Yeah, and if you're so shit-hot, what level are you?" snapped the aggressive guard.

"Firstly, fuck you very much, and secondly,

fuck you some more," snapped Cash. "I'm starting to get a little pissed at your attitude, sonny. So, here's what's gonna happen," he turned to Tom. "You are gonna tell your people to listen to me. I'm gonna make you all an offer. If you lot have any fucking common sense whatsoever, you will accept my help, and then we'll take it from there. Now, lead the way."

The aggressive guard pointed his spear at Cash in a threatening manner. "You don't tell us what to do."

Cash sighed. "As I always say," he said to Bonny. "There's always one asshole." Then he unleashed a small bolt of electricity at the offender. The man went down like he'd been tazed. The shock was enough to incapacitate him, but not powerful enough to do any permanent damage. "Next person who points a weapon at me, is not going to get off so lightly, understand?"

There was a collective nodding of heads.

"Good, now, let's go chat to your people."

CHAPTER 10

Cash led the way as the group moved towards the center of the town hall, where the subdued survivors huddled together, their eyes wide with a mixture of fear and curiosity. A low hum of murmurs filled the air as they whispered among themselves, unsure of what to make of this new and unexpected turn of events.

Bonny stayed close to Cash's side, her presence both a comforting reassurance and a subtle warning to anyone who might consider causing trouble. With a stern expression, Cash addressed the gathering, his voice projecting authority and genuine concern.

Tom called the people to order and then introduced Cash as, a stranger who wants to offer us help. It wasn't the most rousing of introductions, but Cash didn't really care. He wasn't into bigging himself up at any rate.

"Listen up, everyone," he called out, and the room fell silent. "You may have heard the System announcements of late that mentioned me. My name is Cash Stone, the System calls me Lord Appalachia. It's a load of crap, but nevertheless, because of the title I've been gifted with some powers that allow me to help human survivors."

There was a subdued ripple of conversation as various people confirmed their knowledge of Cash's status. Some looked awestruck, others remained blank, and a few even looked at Cash with undisguised disgust. Or perhaps it was fear.

"I won't waste your time with empty promises or false hope," continued Cash. "You've been through hell, and it's clear that you've endured more than your fair share of hardship. But I'm here to offer you a chance to start anew, to find safety and security in a place where we take care of our own. I currently am the Liege-lord of a capital city fairly close by. It's called Tomahawk. It's well protected, there's accommodation, water and power. And I want to extend an invitation to you all to allow me to take you there. You will be well treated and I promise, things will be a lot better."

Many of the people began to talk amongst themselves. But Cash noticed that some of them appeared to be so weak, either through illness or simple malnourishment, that they just sat, still and unresponsive apart from the odd cough.

Cash strode across the room and knelt next to a young girl who appeared to be one of the most ill. She shrank back from him, fear evident in her eyes.

"Don't be scared, little one," said Cash as he

leaned forward and placed his right hand on her shoulder. "I'm just going to cast a healing spell on you. It won't hurt, okay."

With that, Cash cast the spell. The effect was instant, the girl's skin went from pale to healthy, her cheeks filled out and her entire posture changed as she sat up straighter.

Then Cash took out a couple of peaches from his Inventory. Even though they were a few weeks old, the magical space had kept them as fresh as the day he was given them. After that, he took out his water canteen and handed it to the girl. "Eat, drink," he said as he moved on to the next person.

He had to wait for the standard cool down time between each casting, but within a few minutes, he had healed five of the more seriously ill and handed them a combination of peaches, water and jerky.

The room buzzed with conversation as the townsfolk looked upon what appeared to them to be a miracle. The stranger had simply laid his hands upon the sick and healed them.

"Mister," said Tom, his voice filled with awe. "Are you some kind of saint?"

Cash laughed. "Quite the opposite," he said. "I'm actually a grade A, asshole. Seriously, I do this sorta shit because I know it's the right thing to do. But if it were up to me, I probably wouldn't do it at all. If that makes any sense."

Tom faced the room. "Look," he said. "I dunno about you all, but what Lord Appalachia has just done has convinced me. I say we take him up on his offer."

"What's the catch?" asked one of the townsfolk. "There's always a catch."

Tom turned to Cash and raised a questioning eyebrow.

"You're correct," admitted Cash. "The only way I can protect you, is if you swear an oath to become a vassal of mine. But before you say anything, let me tell you. Firstly, I didn't make that rule up. Fact is, I think it's stupid. But the System insists. And secondly, I also have to swear an oath to you. So basically, we both just say that we aren't gonna be assholes. It's pretty simple."

"What's the oath?" asked Tom.

In answer, Cash brought the oath up and transferred it to everyone's HUD's.

Vassal Oath –

I promise on my honor that I will be faithful to my lord. When he calls, I shall come. When he orders, I shall obey. Neither by word, nor deed, nor action shall I betray his trust. And always, in his benefit, shall I act.

Liege Oath –

By my word, ax and honor shall I protect my vassal. Their pain shall be mine to suffer. Their success shall be feted in my halls. When they are in danger, I shall protect them. When they are in need, they may come to me for a surcease. And always, for their benefit, shall my actions lead.

"Doesn't seem that onerous," said Tom. "I'm still in."

"If it means my family and I get clean water, food and protection from the monsters, I'm also in," called out one of the men.

There was a general mutter of agreement.

"Right then," said Cash. "Just read off the oath, I'll say my bit, then we can plan on getting you all to Tomahawk and safety."

As soon as the oaths were finished, Higgins appeared next to Cash.

"Woah, what the hell," yelled Tom along with a chorus of similar exclamations from all present.

"Sorry, this is my AI assistant," explained Cash. "The System provided me with him. Long story, not necessary to go through it right now. Anyway, what is it, Higgins?"

"Two people have not taken the oath," he stated.

"Who?"

Higgins pointed towards an old woman and a young man in his late teens.

Cash walked up to them. The teenager stepped back, his eyes downcast. But the old woman stuck her chin out belligerently and squared up.

"Hey," Cash said. "I know that some folks are a bit nervous of taking the oath. But as you can see, everyone else took it, and they haven't died or nothing, so you can most likely assume it's safe."

"We ain't swearing no oath to you," snapped

the old lady. "And step back, you evil son of a bitch."

Cash frowned but didn't react.

"Glenda, don't you think that's a bit uncalled for," said Tom.

"I know what I see," snapped the old lady. "Calling on dark powers to allegedly heal the sick. You trying to tell me he hasn't stolen their souls? Bullshine, Thomas. Now he's got you all to swear to be his slaves. No, me and Steven want none of that. Mark my words, that man is evil to the core."

Cash looked at the teenager. "Hey, son," he said. "You sure you wanna be a part of this? Maybe you have a talk to you mom here…"

Grandmother," interjected the teenager.

"Okay, grandmother. Listen, son, you don't swear, I can't help you. Seriously, if I could I would, But the System won't let you stay in any of my towns. It's totally fucked up, but it is what it is,"

The teenager shook his head. "I'm sorry."

"You stay here, you will die," said Cash.

"The Lord will protect us," said Glenda. "He will watch over us and defend us from the likes of you." The old lady made the sign of the cross and started mumbling a prayer.

Cash took a deep breath. "Listen you old mental case. Personally, I don't give a flying fuck about you. You're obviously off your rocker. But you carry on like this and you are going to be responsible for the death of your grandson."

"Get the hence, servant of Beelzebub."

"Oh for fuck sakes," sighed Cash. "Higgins, is there any way around this? Can't we find a way to bend the rules? Maybe I can make like a small outpost here for them or something."

Higgins shook his head. "I am afraid not, sir. The System is very strict about this. They swear, or they stay."

Cash ran a hand through his hair. "Okay, look, we'll leave tomorrow at sunup, Tom, see of you can talk some sense into old lady fuckwit here. I'm going to patrol the perimeter with Bonny."

Tom nodded as he watched Cash leave with his canine companion and his AI assistant.

***

The next morning the survivors readied themselves for the trip. They didn't carry much, because they didn't actually possess much.

Cash tried one more time to convince Glenda to swear the oath, but his attempts were to no avail, resulting only in more insults and religious dogma.

"Hey, kid," he said to Glenda's grandson. "I'm sorry. Look, if the old nutcase kicks the bucket, you make your way to Tomahawk, okay."

The teenager nodded, but looked away.

"Fuck," shouted Cash in frustration. "Right, let's move. I'll take the lead, Bonny will follow up the rear. Keep together. Let's move out."

CHAPTER 11

"Son of a bitch," yelled Cash.

"What's the problem?" asked Sarah.

"Those douche-canoe RPG Lords have bumped my Charisma up a point to 9."

"So."

"So, I already told you, I do not want to become mister warm-and-fuzzy. It's a fucking useless stat meant for bunny huggers and politicians."

"Firstly, lord muckamuck," said Sarah. "Your Charisma is still in single figures, so while you're no longer Typhoid-Mary, you still rank somewhere below the homeless bum who crashes a bar mitzvah. And secondly, if you are going to insist on saving random strangers like that last bunch, your Charisma is going to crawl up. Tough, suck it up, buttercup."

"That's Lord Buttercup to you, my lady."

Before either of the two friends could continue their banter, Greta entered the hall.

Cash leaned back in his chair and propped his cybernetic legs up on the table. "So, are those survivors I brought back all settled in then?" he drawled, eyeing the stack of papers in Greta's hands.

"Of course." Greta sniffed, dropping the files onto his desk with a thud. "I've assigned housing, duties, and provisions for the new survivors, as always."

Her pale eyes glinted with determination as she straightened her shoulders, hands clasped behind her back like a general addressing her troops.

Cash bit back a smirk, rolling his eyes when she glanced away. Trust Greta to run Tomahawk like a well-oiled machine.

Still, he couldn't fault her results. Things were going from strength to strength, and without Greta's ruthless efficiency, they'd just be scraping by.

"Good work." He cleared his throat, dropping his boots to the floor. "What're the highlights?"

"We've gained six able-bodied fighters, an engineer with mechanical skills, and a nurse with minor healing powers." Greta ticked off each point on her fingers. "The fighters have integrated well with Gunny's unit. The engineer will work maintaining our defenses. And the nurse will assist Doc in the infirmary."

"Any troublemakers?" Sarah asked, perched on the edge of his desk. Her brow furrowed, tapping her fingers against the hilt of her dagger.

"A few grumblers, but nothing I couldn't handle." Greta's lips twisted into a grim smile, and Cash didn't doubt that for a second. "They'll learn or leave. Simple as that."

"Good to know we're in capable hands." Cash snorted, saluting Greta with two fingers.

She sniffed again but didn't hide her pleased smile, inclining her head in acknowledgment. "Just doing my duty."

With that, Greta spun on her heel and marched from his office, no doubt already calculating how best to integrate the next group of sorry souls to stumble through their gates.

Cash scrubbed a hand over his face, fatigue etching lines into his skin. They'd gained more people, more resources - all while holding back the tide of threats battering at their gates.

"We need to expand." The words came unbidden, spilling from his lips. "We got the space, but we need more bodies. And more towns if we're gonna make our mark before the Integration. And that's only four months away now."

"You're talking about an expedition." Sarah's eyes lit up, a fierce grin curving her mouth "You'll need a team." Sarah slipped from the desk to stand beside him, her shoulder brushing his. "Someone to watch your six. You know I'm with you every step of the way."

"We'll need more than just us." Cash sighed, scrubbing a hand over the back of his neck. "Fighters, scouts, a healer. I wanna go large. Well, large-ish. . Not sure if we should look at a bunch of Adventurers, or Peacekeepers. I'm leaning towards a more military type setup than an Adventurer one. I am army after all. But we'll have to leave enough behind to defend the walls"

"So, we handpick the best, and the rest can damn well hold down the fort until we get back." Sarah bumped her hip against his, a wicked grin pulling at her lips.

"Yeah, yeah." Cash sighed again, staring into the distance as plans and strategies spun through his mind. "Okay, I suppose there's no time like the present and all that crap."

With a resigned sigh, Cash set off to find Gunny. Time to get this show on the road, whether he was ready or not. The world wasn't going to explore itself, and the fate of all the human survivors in the surrounding area depended on what Cash could achieve before the final integration.

No pressure or anything. Cash stifled a groan, running a hand over his face. Just another day in the life of a reluctant hero. The things he did for these people...

But one look at the town, bustling with activity even now, was enough to strengthen his resolve. They'd gotten this far, and he'd be damned if anything stopped them now.

***

Cash found Gunny barking orders at a squad of soldiers, directing them in setting up defensive positions around the fort.

"My lord!" Gunny snapped a salute, expression

grim. "What can I do for you?"

"At ease." Cash waved him off. "I've decided to take a mixed group on a fact-finding mission, look for survivors, maybe take a few more towns under our wing. Big stuff, Gunny. I was thinking a dozen dudes, or dudettes. And there has to be at least one healer. Got any recommendations?"

"Any reason you wanna go for Peacekeepers and not Adventurers? asked Gunny.

Cash shrugged. "Show of force. Not sure actually, I just thought that I want to portray discipline and solidarity to anyone we come across. Adventurers tend to be a bit like me. You know, tending towards the flakey."

Gunny flashed a rare smile. "You said it, sir, not me. I'll put together a squad right away. Anything else?"

"Yeah, make sure they got supplies and extra kit. We'll be gone for at least a week, maybe longer. They need to be prepared for anything."

"Understood. I'll get them equipped and briefed." Gunny paused, gaze flickering over Cash's shoulder. "You're taking the girl, I assume?"

Cash didn't bother turning to look. He knew Sarah had followed him, as she often did. "Yeah. She's proven herself more than capable."

"That she has." There was a grudging note of approval in Gunny's tone. "You've got good instincts, picking them. The men respect her, and she's got skills for days."

"And she's also got a name," snapped Sarah. But

her ire was short lived. She knew Gunny meant nothing bad by referring to her as, the girl. He called everyone, girls or boys. It was his way.

"Tell me something I don't know," Cash muttered. "She's a pain in the ass, but she knows stuff," he concluded with a grin."

"One more thing." Gunny lowered his voice. "You watch your back out there, sir. Tomahawk needs you."

"Duly noted." Cash sighed, running a hand through his hair. "I'll do my best, Gunny. That's all I can promise."

"It's all we need." Gunny snapped another salute. "I'll get the preparations underway."

"Carry on."

As Gunny strode off, barking orders, Sarah came up beside Cash. "So, what's the plan?"

"We head out at first light," Cash said. "You, me, and a team of the best and brightest Tomahawk has to offer. Time to see what the fuck the rest of this area's got in store for us this time."

Sarah grinned, a fierce light in her eyes. "This is going to be fun."

"You and I have very different definitions of fun," Cash said wryly. But despite his grumbling, he had to admit he was looking forward to the challenge. Maybe, just maybe, this expedition wouldn't end in complete disaster.

Stranger things had happened.

***

The residents of Tomahawk were abuzz with anticipation as the team prepared for the journey ahead, driven by their desire to support Cash and the success of the expedition.

The news spread like wildfire. A large, armed expedition, led by none other than Cash Stone himself, with Sarah at his side. The people of Tomahawk stirred with excitement and nerves, a mixture of eagerness and trepidation.

Cash was their leader, their hero, the one who'd helped build their settlement from the ground up. They trusted him to lead them to victory, to explore the unknown and return triumphant. But the RPG world was dangerous, filled with peril at every turn. Lives could be lost, resources wasted. The fate of Tomahawk itself might hang in the balance.

Still, spirits were high as preparations got underway. Supplies were gathered, weapons sharpened, Inventories filled with rations and gear. Anticipation hung thick in the air, fueled by possibility and purpose.

Tomahawk was ready to expand its borders. The surrounding area wouldn't know what hit it.

Cash surveyed the group with a practiced eye, weighing each member's strengths and weaknesses. Gunny had handpicked each volunteer himself. As opposed to an adventuring group made up of Tanks, Rogues, Scouts and Melee warriors, the military group were all very similar.

Apart for the healer, that Gunny referred to as the Field Medic.

Gunny knew every member's skills, their gear, their temperament. He'd forged them into a cohesive unit, one that could adapt to any situation. They were prepared for anything the System might throw at them.

"All right, listen up!" Cash barked, coming to stand before the group. A dozen faces turned his way, snapping to attention. "We'll head out now. Anyone not ready gets left behind. You know your roles, so get to it. Dismissed!"

The team scattered to finish their preparations, a flurry of activity and purpose. Cash watched them go with a surge of pride. They were a good bunch, and he was glad to have them along for this madcap adventure.

Tomahawk's fate, and quite possibly mankind's, rested on their shoulders. But if anyone could get the job done, it was this team.

Cash smiled grimly, cracking his knuckles. "Let's do this."

CHAPTER 12

The dimly lit boardroom buzzed with an electric atmosphere as the System Overlords settled their bets on Cash Stone. Piles of credits exchanged hands, transferring ownership with each transaction. Laughter filled the air, accompanied by the clinking of glasses and boisterous chatter.

One Overlord, a mischievous gleam in their eyes, pocketed a hefty sum, their smirk widening with satisfaction. "Yes! Take that!" they cackled triumphantly.

Another cursed under their breath, reluctantly handing over their hard-earned credits to their victorious counterpart. "You got lucky this time," they murmured grudgingly.

The room became a swirling sea of wagers and exchanges, as the Overlords reveled in their macabre game of chance.

Amidst the revelry, the senior Overlord, his presence commanding respect, rose to his feet. The room fell into an expectant hush as all eyes turned to him.

"My esteemed colleagues," he began, his voice

commanding attention. "While our bets have provided us with ample amusement, I believe it is time to increase the stakes. We need more suffering, more trials for our dear Cash Stone. The entertainment value must be intensified."

A murmur of agreement swept through the room, excitement mingling with a hint of sadistic pleasure. The Overlords, driven by their insatiable hunger for amusement, craved greater challenges for their unwitting player.

"Indeed," another Overlord chimed in, their voice tinged with anticipation. "Let us raise the difficulty, present him with trials that will push him to his limits. The greater the struggle, the sweeter the victory, or in this case, the agony."

Laughter erupted, echoing off the obsidian walls as the Overlords reveled in their wicked intentions. Some proposed traps and puzzles that would test Cash's wit and ingenuity, while others suggested hordes of powerful adversaries to overwhelm him.

The senior Overlord, a twisted smile etching itself upon his features, raised a hand to silence the room. His eyes gleamed with a mixture of malevolence and anticipation.

"Let it be known," he declared, his voice carrying the weight of their collective authority, "that Cash Stone shall face trials more formidable than ever before. We shall weave a web of challenges that will push him to the brink, where every victory is earned through sweat, blood, and sacrifice."

The room erupted in applause, the sound a cacophony of twisted delight. The Overlords, intoxicated by their power and control, reveled in their ability to manipulate the fates of their players.

As the meeting adjourned, the Overlords dispersed, each consumed by their own visions of torment and tormenting. They busied themselves with preparations, plotting and scheming to create a labyrinth of suffering for Cash Stone, a maze from which escape seemed impossible.

Meanwhile, the fate of Cash Stone hung in the balance, unbeknownst to him. The game had escalated, its challenges sharpened to deadly precision. As Cash prepared to face the next trial, little did he know that the Overlords had conspired to unleash a storm upon him, where pain and despair would become his closest companions.

In the shadows, the Overlords reveled in their wicked amusement, their laughter echoing through the hollow corridors of power. They relished the impending battles, eagerly anticipating the spectacle that would unfold in the realm they controlled.

With each passing moment, the stage was set, and the players moved into position. The fate of Cash Stone and the destiny of the world intertwined, bound by the whims of these malevolent puppet masters. In this twisted game of life and death, the price of survival was immeasurable, and the price of failure, absolute.

CHAPTER 13

With a grunt, Cash stood up and stretched. They had walked hard the day before and set up camp as the sun was slipping below the horizon. The Lieutenant, Jack Pension, a man in his thirties, had organized the watch schedule, and even though Cash and Sarah had volunteered to be part of the roster, Jack had simply shaken his heads, like the very suggestion was insane. "No lords or ladies on watch," he said.

Cash didn't argue, he supposed that being Lord Appalachia should have some perks, because on the whole it was a plentiful pain in the butt.

Cash pulled out his canteen and downed some water. Moments later, one of the soldiers marched up and handed him a lump of cheese and a heel of bread.

"Thanks, soldier."

The soldier saluted. "Yes, sir!"

Cash snorted, waving a hand. "At ease. None of that 'sir' nonsense."

Though he'd never admit it aloud, Cash felt a surge of pride as he watched the Peacekeepers assemble. They were a professional looking bunch, with matching armor, rectangular shields, spears and a short sword on their belts.

"Ready to march, my lord!" the lieutenant stood at attention, back straight and hand on the hilt of his sword.

Cash shook off his reverie. "Right. Let's get a move on."

They headed north along the remains of what only a short time ago had been a major road. But the onset of the System apocalypse had hastened the collapse of all pre-apocalyptic structures. The remnants of the blacktop wound through abandoned farms and empty fields. Skeletons of long-dead vehicles littered the roadside, rusting reminders of the old world.

Cash kept his gaze roving, as he scanned for any signs of movement.

Bonny trotted at Cash's side, her keen nose sniffing the air. The Tamaskan let out a warning growl, hackles rising as she peered into the overgrown brush.

Cash tensed, reflexively equipping his crossbow out. "What is it, girl?"

Before Bonny could respond, a shriek rang out. A hulking figure burst from the bushes, brandishing a rusted machete.

The Peacekeepers ran forwards, unslinging their shields and linking together to form a shieldwall in front of their Lord.

Cash used Identify on the massive bipedal

creature.

Mutant Gorilla - *Level 25*
HP *300/300*
Weakness - *Not the fastest thinker*
Strength – *Berserker*

The mutant was nearly twelve feet tall, with twisted limbs and a grotesque bulging cranium. Foam flecked its lips as it charged straight toward them, madness burning in its eyes.

"Look out!" Sarah yanked a vial from her bandolier, hurling it over the shieldwall and at the mutant's feet.

The vial shattered, releasing a noxious green cloud. The mutant stumbled into the cloud with a roar, then ground to a halt, coughing and retching violently.

Cash let out a low whistle. "Nice throw."

"Learned from the best." Sarah smiled, brushing a lock of hair from her eyes.

"Wall, two ranks, hold," the lieutenant ordered.

The line of Peacekeepers changed their formation, moving to two ranks of six. The rear rank held their shields higher and rested their spears on the top rim of the shields. The first rank stood firm, shields interlocked, spears held forward.

Before the Mutant Gorilla recovered from its coughing fit, Jack yelled out another order.

"Advance and engage."

With a shared war cry, the Peacekeepers took

two steps forward, and as the Mutant came into range, they thrust their spears forward.

The Gorilla went from coughing mutant to pincushion in a split second.

"Again," bellowed Jack.

The spears withdrew and then lunged forward once more. This time the Mutant leaped towards them. A move that did it no good whatsoever as the wide bladed spears struck hard and deep, opening a series of massive wounds in the creature's flesh.

Sarah started winding up a magma missile to finish the mob off, but Cash stopped her.

"Wait," he suggested. "Let's see how they handle this."

As it happened the end was almost anticlimactic. Lieutenant Jack simply drew his short sword, stepped over to the now prone mutant and with a mighty lunge drove the blade into the back of its head.

The creature spasmed a couple of time and then went still.

Then with a few economical gestures Jack sent six of the Peacekeepers into the surrounding forest in pairs to search for any more possible mobs.

Cash walked up to the officer and nodded his appreciation. "Nice work," he praised. "Very efficient. Tell me, do any of you guys have ranged spells, ranged weapons? Or do you have to get close up and personal every time?"

"With bigger squads we have crossbows and

some troops with ranged spells," informed Jack. "But Gunny figured that you and Lady Sarah would have that side of things covered. So we went with the setup we got now. Although, Lady Sarah did make these for us." Jack pulled a glass contained from his Inventory. "Fire grenades. I have no idea what's in them, but you chuck them at the enemy, they explode on contact and there's fire everywhere."

Cash grinned. "Sarah does like to burn shit down."

The scouts arrived back and informed Jack that the area was clear.

"Well done, guys." Cash clapped Jack on the shoulder, then gazed northward. According to his maps, they were only a few miles from the next town. "Let's pick up the pace. We've got survivors to save."

The Peacekeepers quickened their steps, marching in tight formation with Cash at the lead. Bonny let out an excited bark, tail wagging.

Up ahead, the ruins of an old diner came into view, neon sign broken and dull. And beyond that, the remains of what was most likely a fairly decent post-apocalyptic wall only a few days before. The scars and holes in the structure were fresh enough that they hadn't yet been affected by the weather or plant growth.

"Looks like something hit that wall hard in the last couple of days," ventured Cash.

Both Jack and Sarah nodded their agreement.

As the group entered the ruins of the town, Cash signaled for the Peacekeepers to fan out. He peered around each corner and into every building, mana crossbow at the ready, but the place seemed deserted.

"Hello?" He called out as they walked down the main street. "We come in peace. Just looking to help."

Silence.

Then a shutter creaked behind them. Cash whirled around, training his crossbow on the source of the sound, but it was just a stray gust of wind.

"Place seems dead," said Jack. "Should we return to camp?"

Cash was about to agree when a flicker of movement caught his eye. A young boy peered out from behind an old pickup truck, eyes wide with terror.

"There," Cash said, raising his hands in a peaceful gesture. "We mean you no harm."

The boy didn't move. Cash took a slow step forward and gave him his friendliest smile. "My name's Cash. What's your name?"

The boy swallowed hard. "T-Ty."

"It's okay, Ty. We're here to help." Cash glanced over his shoulder at the Peacekeepers, who had formed a defensive circle around Sarah and Higgins. "My friends and I, we're trying to unite the towns around here. Create a safe zone. Make sure everyone has food and shelter."

Ty peered up at him with a mix of hope and skepticism. "You're...not gonna raid us?"

"No raids. No violence. Just safety, security, and a brighter future." Cash extended his flesh and blood hand. "We've come from the town of Tomahawk. We can show you how it's prospering now, if you'd like to see for yourself."

Ty hesitated, then slid out from behind the pickup truck. He walked over to Cash and placed his hand in the larger, calloused one.

"Deal," Ty said.

Cash grinned. "Welcome to the empire, kid. Now, tell me, where is everyone else? And what the hell happened here?"

Ty frowned. "Everyone is dead, or the Marauders took them."

"The Marauders?"

"A gang of bad people," answered Ty. "They attacked us a couple of days ago. Then some of the men who lived here turned on us. They opened the gates. I ran and hid. They had dogs...sorta dogs, who tracked everyone down. Most they killed, some they took with them. I hid in the sewers. The dog monsters couldn't smell me. I'm hungry and thirsty."

"Oh, shit, sorry kid," said Cash as he took some bread and a water canteen from his Inventory. Ty grabbed the bread and wolfed it down.

***

Cash led the squad through the broken town, ax in

hand. His cybernetic limbs hummed with power, ready to strike at a moment's notice. Bonny stalked at his side, her lips curled back from her teeth.

The town square was deserted. Shutters hung open and crooked on their hinges, creaking in the wind. Stalls sat abandoned, rotten fruit and spoiled meat crawling with flies. A foul stench hung in the air, the unmistakable reek of death.

"Over here," one of the Peacekeepers called. He was kneeling beside a body lying face down in the dirt, covered in dried blood. More bodies were scattered throughout the square, slumped against walls or lying in the street. Men, women, even a few children. None had survived.

Cash swore under his breath. "Check the houses," he ordered. "See if anyone's left alive."

The Peacekeepers dispersed, weapons at the ready. Cash did a slow turn, surveying the carnage. This had been wholesale slaughter. Straight up mass murder.

Ty had called the attackers, the Marauders. Cash wondered what their end game was. Were they looking to expand their territory, or were they simply like the Vikings of old, raping and pillaging wherever they went.

One by one, the Peacekeepers returned, shaking their heads. The town was dead.

"We should move on," Sarah said softly. "There's nothing we can do for these poor souls now."

Cash ground his teeth as anger rose within him

like a tsunami. "The Marauders must pay for this," he said, his voice a low growl. "Bonny, you reckon you can track these fuckers?"

Bonny looked up at her master and nodded. "Arf!"

"Do it," grunted Cash. "it's kick ass time."

CHAPTER 14

The Marauders were camped in a valley, celebrating their latest conquest. Over a hundred bandits, heavily armed and armored, weapons glinting in the firelight.

From his position on a nearby ridge, Cash surveyed them through a pair of binoculars. He'd spent hours observing their patrols and defenses, looking for weaknesses to exploit.

"They outnumber us almost eight-to-one," noted Sarah. "Maybe we should send for reinforcements."

Cash shook his head. "They're all Level 3 to 5. Only their leader and his deputy are over Level 10. We don't need reinforcements, and we don't really need much of a plan. We just go down there and kill these murderous fuckers."

"Look, mister fancy-pants Lord," quipped Sarah. "I'm sure you could probably take them by yourself, but before you let your anger get the best of you, remember there are innocent prisoners, slaves serving them, women, children. For fuck sakes, Cash, you were a Ranger, you can come up with some sort of plan that doesn't involve putting all those innocents at risk."

Cash stared at his friend, then he had the good grace to look a little embarrassed. "You're right," he admitted. "Give me a few minutes to think."

***

Cash outlined the plan to his men. A small team of six Peacekeepers would sneak into the camp, killing any guards they came across on the way. Then they would enter any tents that contained sleeping bandits and dispatch them using a variety of Sarah's various poisonous potions. She only had a few of them, but she assured the Peacekeepers that one per tent would be enough to incapacitate anyone inside.

Obviously, the soldiers would have to finish the job with cold steel.

As soon as they infiltrators had done what they could, Cash and the rest of the force would charge down the ridge and attack.

There was a brief pause and then Sarah shook her head, a slight smile on her lips. "You know," she said. "That plan is hardly any different to your first plan of just run at them and kill them all."

Cash shrugged. "I added a bit of subterfuge."

"May I add one small suggestion?" interjected Sarah.

"Sure."

"The prisoners seem to be mainly kept in that stockade on the right of the camp. What say, Bonny, Higgins and I slip over there when the fun starts and protect them from any friendly fire. Also, maybe we can free them and get them all out of harm's way. Plus Higgins can keep watch for us so Bonny and I can concentrate on taking down bad guys."

Cash grinned. "Good plan, batman."

"Batman?"

"You don't like Batman? Fine, Higgins can be Batman, whatever, go for it. The rest of you ready?"

Jack nodded and got his team of assassins to begin their slow, careful crawl towards the camp. The rest of them waited, mentally preparing themselves for the battle ahead.

The night air crackled with anticipation as Cash and his remaining forces crouched in the cover of the ridge. The moon cast a pale glow upon the bandit camp below, revealing the flickering torches and the hushed murmurs of the criminals.

Cash used his superior night vision to keep track of the six Peacekeepers that were infiltrating the camp. They were moving slowly, trading stealth for speed. But that was best, time wasn't a factor. They had all night.

Two, then three, then finally seven guards were taken out. Short swords cutting throats, and then bodies laid gently down, pushed into the shadows to avoid exposure.

Then they were amongst the bandits' tents. It was immediately apparent which of the tents contained sleeping bandits as they were dark and quiet.

The Peacekeepers split into teams of two. Then they approached a tent, pulled the opening softly aside, and tossed in one of Sarah's alchemic potions. Sarah had told them the potions were fast acting and dissipated extremely quickly. So the counted off a full minute, then slipped inside, swords ready. It was bloody work, but it was necessary.

The minutes ticked down. After ten more minutes, the teams had killed over twenty guards. They were doing incredibly well, but in a combat situation, one's luck is a finite thing. And as the one duo opened the flap to the fifth tent, a bandit inside yelled out.

Cash decided the game was up and chose that moment to attack.

Casting a lightning bolt at the group of bandits sitting around the main central fire, he broke into a sprint.

"Let's get the fuckers," he cried out, loosing bolt after bolt from his mana crossbow as he closed in on the group of almost eighty heavily armed bandits.

The Peacekeepers formed up, joining the six who had snuck in previously, and they formed a tightly linked shield wall, spears forward as the advanced.

Sarah and Bonny, their forms blending into the darkness, stealthily made their way towards the stockade where the captured prisoners were held. Their movements were precise and deliberate, their senses sharp as they navigated through the shadows. With each step, they drew closer to their objective, ready to protect the defenseless and set them free from their captors.

Meanwhile, Cash's heart pounded in his chest, a mix of adrenaline and determination coursing through his veins. He gripped his ax tightly, feeling the raw power of the lightning spells pulsating within him. He glanced at his men, their expressions a mix of nerves and resolve, knowing that their lives depended on the success of this assault.

Battle cries echoed through the night. The bandits, fought back, using their superior numbers in an attempt to overwhelm the small group of highly trained Peacekeepers.

The clash of steel reverberated through the camp as the Peacekeepers engaged the bandits in close combat. Swords clashed against swords, shields locked in a test of strength. The Peacekeepers fought with discipline and precision, their training evident in every strike and parry.

Meanwhile, Cash unleashed his lightning spells with devastating precision. Bolts of electricity crackled through the air, finding their marks and sending bandits sprawling to the ground. The smell of singed flesh mingled with the acrid scent of smoke as flames erupted from the fallen enemies. It was a display of raw power, an exhibition of magic that left both friend and foe in awe.

As the chaos unfolded, Sarah, Higgins and Bonny reached the stockade. With a flick of her wrist, Sarah unleashed a fireball, incinerating the lock that held the prisoners captive. The gates swung open, and the captives stumbled out, their eyes wide with a mix of fear and relief. Sarah and Bonny guided them away from the heat of battle, ushering them towards safety.

With the prisoners freed and the bandits faltering under the relentless assault, Cash's rage ignited. He let out a primal roar, a feral growl escaping his lips as he charged into the midst of the enemy, his ax held high. His strikes were swift and deadly, his every movement a dance of carnage and destruction.

Bandits fell left and right as Cash unleashed his pent-up fury upon them. Their screams of pain and fear filled the night air, a macabre symphony that underscored his relentless assault. It was a sight that struck fear into the hearts of his own men, who watched in awe and trepidation as their lord became an unstoppable force of nature.

In a matter of minutes, Cash had singlehandedly decimated over fifty bandits, leaving behind a trail of broken bodies in his wake. The surviving bandits, their spirits shattered and their will to fight extinguished, threw down their weapons and surrendered.

With the battle won, Cash stood amidst the carnage, his breath ragged and his body covered in the blood of his enemies. His men approached cautiously, their expressions a mix of admiration and a hint of fear. They had witnessed firsthand the savagery and brutality that lurked within their lord, and it left them in awe.

"You did it, my lord," Jack said, his voice filled with reverence. "You... you were terrible to behold."

Cash exhaled, his chest heaving, as he looked upon the defeated bandits and the chaos that surrounded him. He nodded to his men, his eyes reflecting a mix of weariness and satisfaction. "Secure the prisoners," he ordered, his voice carrying the weight of command. "We will take them back to Tomahawk and ensure they face justice for their crimes. I want word to spread, banditry will not be tolerated."

As the Peacekeepers moved to carry out his orders, Cash's gaze shifted to the horizon, his mind already focused on the next challenge that awaited him. But first he had to get this lot home and integrated into his burgeoning new community.

CHAPTER 15

As the group made their way back to Tomahawk, the air was thick with a sense of relief. The survivors they had rescued were weary but grateful, their tired faces displaying a glimmer of hope.

The peaceful journey was abruptly interrupted as a thunderous growl echoed through the forest. The ground trembled beneath their feet, and before they could react, a massive pack of Swarmbeasts emerged from the dense foliage. Their chitinous armor gleamed in the dappled sunlight, and their razor-sharp claws scraped against the earth, filling the air with an eerie sound. Some were flying, their too-small wings causing them to veer erratically across the sky, while other kept to the ground.

Cash quickly used Identify.

***Swarmbeast** – Level 15*
***HP** - 150*
***Strength** – Swarm attack*
***Weakness** – Physical attack*

He flicked his attention to a few other beasts and

saw their levels varied between 15 and 20. And there were loads of them. This was not going to be easy.

The Peacekeepers sprang into action, forming a defensive line with their shields raised and spears at the ready. Cash and Sarah took a step forward, their hands charged with magical energy. Sarah unleashed a torrent of fireballs, engulfing several Swarmbeasts in roaring flames. Their insect-like wings flapped frantically as they screeched in pain, but their relentless advance continued.

Cash, his heart pounding in his chest, summoned bolts of crackling lightning that arced through the air, striking the Swarmbeasts with deadly precision. But for every one he took down, two more seemed to take its place. The swarm closed in, overwhelming the group with their sheer numbers and ferocity.

In the midst of the chaos, Cash's worst fear became reality. A Swarmbeast lunged forward, snatching the young boy, Ty, with its jagged claws. Time seemed to slow as Cash watched in horror, his mind racing with a mix of fury and desperation.

Without a second thought, Cash's instincts kicked in. He sprinted towards a nearby tree, his muscles straining with every step. With a burst of adrenaline-fueled strength, he propelled himself into the air, launching towards the Swarmbeast that held Ty captive. The creature let out a screech of surprise as Cash crashed onto its back, his fingers sinking into its chitinous armor. Then he grabbed Ty and swung him onto his own back.

"Hold on, buddy," he yelled as he redoubled his efforts to dispatch the beast.

A battle ensued, a clash of wills between man and beast. Cash's desperation fueled his fury as he tore into the creature with a savagery he didn't know he possessed. His blows landed with brutal force, chipping away at the Swarmbeast's defenses. Ty, wide-eyed with fear, clung onto Cash's back, holding on for dear life.

Finally, after literally tearing one of the beast's wings to shreds, Cash felt them plummet from the sky. He immediately spun Ty to his chest and wrapped his arms around him in an effort to protect him. They crashed through a number of tree branches, but Cash ensured Ty wasn't harmed, and when they hit the ground, the boy was fine, apart from being in total shock.

"Bonny," shouted Cash. "Protect Ty."

The massive Tamaskan sprinted over and dropped down in front of Ty.

"I think she wants you to get on her back," said Cash.

Ty complied, jumping up and grabbing a handful of hair. Bonny grinned wolfishly and then ran off, positioning herself behind the Peacekeepers shield wall.

Meanwhile, Sarah and the Peacekeepers fought valiantly. It didn't help that most of their focus was on protecting the survivors they had just freed. But even though they were doing their utmost, there were still casualties. And already at least five civilians lay still on the ground, their bodies torn and bleeding.

Realizing the dire situation, Cash shouted to his companions, his voice filled with determination. "Retreat! Get to safety!" His eyes burned with a mixture of desperation and resolve as he held off the advancing Swarmbeasts, his body battered and bloodied. "Make sure you get the civilians to Tomahawk. I'll hold them back! Just go!"

"No way," yelled Sarah. "You stay, I stay."

Cash turned to his friend and shook his head. "This is not the time, Sarah," he said. "For once, just fucking do as I say. I need you to protect those people. And I won't have the time to watch your back while I'm fighting. So go, now. Bonny, you too,"

Bonny nodded and Jack threw a quick salute in Cash's direction as he turned to organize his people and get them the hell outa Dodge.

As they withdrew, all of them cast worried glances back at Cash, their hearts heavy with the knowledge that he was risking everything to protect them.

Higgins, his usual composed demeanor most definitely off kilter, remained by Cash's side. "Sir, this is post-integration mob behavior," he informed, his voice tinged with concern.

"Something is amiss. The strength and coordination they exhibit... it's unnatural. A wave of this nature should not be occurring at this point in time."

Cash barely registered the words, his focus solely on the horde of Swarmbeasts before him. "Yeah, not natural," he quipped. "In case you hadn't noticed, Higgins, I'm being attacked by flying, armored, beasty, insect fucking monsters. Nothing about this situation is natural."

"True, sir," responded Higgins. "I suppose this isn't the best time to discuss perceived abnormalities vis-à-vis the timelines involved."

"Higgy-baby..."

"Yes, sir. I know. Shut the fuck up."

Cash fought with a desperation born from the need to save the innocent, ignoring the pain that surged through his body with every strike he delivered and every wound he received. Time seemed to blur as he became a whirlwind of fury, holding off the Swarmbeasts with sheer determination.

Summoning the last reserves of his willpower, Cash dredged up his last reserves of energy, his body trembling with exhaustion. A fire ignited within him, a fierce resolve that defied the odds. With a roar that echoed through the battlefield, he unleashed a final burst of lightning, channeling all his remaining magical energy into one devastating attack.

The Swarmbeasts faltered, their movements

slowed as the electricity coursed through their armored bodies. It was a brief reprieve, but it was enough. In the precious moments that followed, Cash fought with the desperation of a cornered animal. He swung his ax with a ferocity that defied logic, each strike a testament to his unwavering determination.

Swarmbeast after Swarmbeast fell under Cash's relentless assault, their chitinous bodies shattered and broken. The battlefield became a whirlwind of chaos, as if the elements themselves were awed by the sheer force of his will. Cash used his Teleport spell to dodge and attack from differing directions, but soon stopped as it was confusing him as much as the Swarmbeasts. The surviving Swarmbeasts retreated, their once-unyielding advance now reduced to scattered remnants.

As the dust settled, Cash found himself on his knees once more, his body battered and bruised, his breath coming in ragged gasps. He looked around, his eyes scanning the field of fallen foes. The ground was littered with the lifeless forms of the Swarmbeasts, their threat finally vanquished.

But amidst the victory, a wave of pain and exhaustion washed over Cash. The toll of the battle hit him with full force, his battered body unable to withstand the strain any longer. His vision blurred, and his senses dulled as darkness threatened to consume him.

Just as he thought he couldn't hold on any

longer, a familiar voice cut through the haze. "Cash! Cash, are you alright?" It was Sarah, her voice laced with concern as she rushed to his side, her eyes widening at the sight of his battered form.

Cash managed a weak smile, his voice a mere whisper. "I thought I told you to go back to Tomahawk."

"You did, but knowing your occasional penchant for being an idiot, I ignored you. Well, not at first, but after a short while I decided to come back for you."

"Thanks," mumbled Cash. "I'm... I'm okay, Sarah. Just... need a moment." He reached out to her, his hand trembling, and she took it in hers, offering a reassuring squeeze.

As the adrenaline subsided, Cash's body slowly began to recover. His wounds, though painful, were not life-threatening, and his mana gradually replenished. With Sarah's support, he found the strength to stand once more, and as his mana refilled, he cast Healing on himself, increasing his recovery rate dramatically.

Together, they made their way back to Tomahawk, the town that had become their sanctuary. The sight that greeted them was nothing short of jubilant. The townsfolk, who had mourned Cash's presumed demise, now erupted into cheers and applause as he stepped through the gates, Sarah at his side.

The refugees, under Bonny's watchful eye, had arrived safely, and tears of relief and joy streamed down their faces. The air was filled with a renewed sense of hope, as if Cash's miraculous survival had breathed new life into their spirits.

The townsfolk approached Cash with gratitude shining in their eyes, their voices a chorus of appreciation. They hailed him as a hero, their savior, for they had believed he had fallen in the battle against the Swarmbeasts. Cash accepted their praise humbly, knowing that it was not his victory alone, but the result of the collective resilience and courage of the entire town.

Amidst the celebration, Cash's gaze met Sarah's, and they shared a silent understanding. Their bond had grown stronger through the trials they had faced together, and they knew that their fight was far from over. The battle against the darkness had only just begun, but with the indomitable spirit of Tomahawk behind them, they were ready to face whatever challenges lay ahead.

As the cheers and jubilation continued, Cash took a moment to reflect. He had stared death in the face, embraced the possibility of his own demise, and emerged victorious. It was a humbling reminder of the fragility of life and the unwavering strength of the human spirit.

With renewed purpose burning within him, Cash Stone stood tall, ready to lead his people into a future where hope triumphed over despair, and where the sacrifices made in the name of protecting the innocent would never be in vain.

***

And in a place that was at once unbelievably distant, yet only light seconds away, hundreds of thousands of credits changed hands.

"Well, that was one for the books," expressed the senior Overlord. "In excess of two hundred Swarmbeasts, and he took them all down."

"In all fairness," interjected a more junior member of the council. "He did have help. Those Peacekeepers have turned out to be rather an efficient force. Very impressive."

"So what next?" questioned yet another Overlord.

The Senior Overlord grinned. "We step it up even more."

There was a general murmur of conversation as bets were placed and strategies discussed. Opinions varied.

But one thing was certain – Cash Stone was not going to be in for a good time.

CHAPTER 16

Cash stood on his balcony, his mind buzzing with the possibilities that his newfound levels and System points brought. He had reached Level 30, a significant milestone in his journey, and the surge of power and knowledge coursed through his veins. His total stats points now amounted to 38, thanks to the combination of his accumulated points and the bonus points granted for reaching level 30.

With a sense of purpose, Cash allocated his points, spreading them evenly apart from Dexterity and of cause Charisma. He snorted in disbelief as he noted that the System had once again increased his Charisma by a point, He was now officially in double digits.

10.

He shook his head. There was no use complaining, after all there was nothing he or anyone could do about it. And he wasn't actually wasting any of his hard-earned points on the stupid stat. All of his Charisma increases were a bonus

Cash knew that his increased Charisma would

bolster the morale of his people, inspiring them to greater heights, so he supposed he shouldn't feel as irritable as he was. In fact, he no longer knew why he got so pissed at the stat.

"Fucking dickwads upped my Charisma again," he said to Higgins. "10 points."

Higgins chuckled. "Do not worry, sir," he answered. "Your natural antagonistic attitude will surely nullify at least fifty percent of those points. Rest assured, sir, most will still consider you to be a rather despicable character."

"Despicable? That's a bit harsh. I was thinking more along the lines of grumpy."

"Oh no, sir, grumpy suits a curmudgeonly grandfather. You are most definitely more of the aggressively cantankerous type."

Cash frowned. "Umm ... thanks?"

"You are welcome, my Lord."

"I've also been allocated a shit load of System points, so I reckon I'm gonna do a few upgrades. Those Swarmbeasts were scary as hell, and we got no weapons that are suitable for aerial defense.

Cash pulled up his HUD. "Hey, Higgins, how do I access what weapons I can get with my System points?"

Higgins took control of Cash's HUD and pulled up the relevant list.

"Cool, thanks." Cash spent a few minutes perusing the list. When it came to wall mounted weapons, they were all basically a variation on the same theme. Catapults or crossbows. They had different names, trebuchets, mangonels, onagers, scorpions, ballistae, and many more.

Cash finally decided on four tower mounted onagers. Basically, a large torsion powered catapult that could fire loads of fist sized stones or even bundles of darts or arrows. He reckoned they would provide good anti-air firepower. But could also be used against ground-based attacks. Then he blew other 20 points on upgrading the walls and adding a moat and drawbridge.

After that, he turned his attention to the town itself, and here his vision for the town extended beyond mere fortifications. Inspired by Sarah's suggestion, he allocated additional points to construct a greenhouse, a haven for alchemic herbs. Its glass panels glimmered under the sunlight, nurturing the growth of potent ingredients that would aid in the creation of powerful potions and remedies.

Greta, ever practical and forward-thinking, had earlier approached Cash with a proposal. She had requested the addition of a professional abattoir, butchery and meat smoking house. She maintained it would allow the town to efficiently process and preserve the game they hunted and ensure a steady supply of food. And Cash saw no downside to the idea, so he added one on the outskirts of the town, next to the wall.

His upgrades complete, Cash decided to visit Gunny and get an update on how the Peacekeepers were progressing. He also wanted to inform the former Marine that he was planning on heading out again soon and if possible, he wanted the same team he had taken the time before.

"Hey, Higgins, where's Bonny?"

"With Ty, sir."

"She's spending a lot of time with him."

"Jealous, sir?"

"Ha ha. No, just wondering if the little guy is okay."

"He appears to be fine, sir. Youth conquers many traumas."

"Cool, I need to catch up with him soon."

"I shall remind you to do so, sir."

It took a few minutes to walk over to the training area and barracks, and when he got there, Gunny was waiting for him, obviously forewarned by one of his sentries.

"Lord Cash, I've gathered another twenty able-bodied men and women who are eager to join the Peacekeepers. And I've been thinking... I see you added a few more catapults to our defense."

"Onagers, actually," corrected Cash.

Gunny raised an eyebrow. "Really? What's the difference?"

Cash shrugged. "Nothing, I suppose. Just the name."

"Well, my lord, onagers then. Frankly, I don't give a flying fuck whatever fancy name you officers come up with. To me they're just catapults. Anyway, I like them. Small enough to be portable. They can use a range of missiles. Easy to reload. Nice weapons. Anyway, with our growing numbers, it might be time to establish an artillery section."

Cash raised an eyebrow, intrigued by the idea. "And you reckon you'd start with a bunch of those catapults?"

"Onagers," corrected Gunny with a blank stare.

Cash laughed. "Touché, Marine. Okay, how many?"

"Let's start with three, and we'll take it from there."

Cash nodded approvingly. "Very well, Gunny. Proceed with the preparations. I'll allocate the points and place the mangonels in your square. Also, I'm aiming on heading out into the field again. Most likely tomorrow. One of the survivors we brought back told me they'd heard of a town with a proper wall and lots of survivors, Up North, a place called Honeydew. Hey, it's most probably just a rumor, but I need to check it out. So, are the same team available? We worked well together."

Gunny nodded. "I'd like to add a team of four arbalists, the reports Lieutenant Jack gave me sounded like a few more ranged options won't go amiss."

"Arbalists?"

"Crossbowmen."

"Ooh, look who's getting all word-smithy on me now."

"With all due respect, my lord," sniffed Gunny. "Fuck off."

Cash laughed. "No worries, Gunny. Off shall I fuck. Got places to go at any rate."

Cash walked out, looking to find Greta. He had another idea he wanted her to sort out.

It took Cash longer to find Greta than he figured it would. Not because he had no idea where she was, after asking a couple of people they had directed him to the System Shop. No, the reason he took so much time was because so many of the townsfolk stopped to talk to him, to greet, to praise, or simply to bow and give their thanks.

"Fucking Charisma stat," mumbled Cash. "I told you this sorta shit would start happening," he whispered to Higgins. "Despicable, my hairy ass. These fuckers love me."

"Do not confuse fear and respect for love, sir," admonished Higgins jokingly. "After all, you do hold their lives in your hands."

"Whatever," muttered Cash. "I'm becoming one lovable SOB."

"Of course, sir. Whatever you say."

Cash saw Greta coming out of the shop as he approached and he greeted her with a smile. "Hey, been shopping?"

"More raw iron for the smithy," she replied. "What can I do you for?"

"Maybe I just wanted to say hi," responded Cash.

"Yeah, and maybe little piggies might fly. Come on, my lord. What?"

"I was thinking of starting some sort of school

for the kids."

"And?"

"And what, I don't have a plan. I'm the ideas guy. You make the plans."

Greta shook her head. "Not sure when I'll fit that in," she said.

"You sleep much?" asked Cash.

"Some."

"Well sleep less," chuckled Cash. "But seriously, Greta, if you need help why don't you get an assistant?"

Greta nodded. "You're right. I'll look into that. Thanks for the abattoir, by the way. That will really help with the meat processing."

"My pleasure," said Cash. "Because, meat is meat and a man must eat. And duck is duck ... and a man must ... eat poultry as well."

Greta shook her head and rolled her eyes. "Hilarious, I'm sure. Look, give me a few days, I'll find someone to handle this school idea. I think it's a good thing."

"I'm outa here tomorrow," said Cash. "But as always, I have full confidence in you."

"Take care, my lord," said Greta. "Don't get killed. We need you."

Cash gave her a wink and left, heading back to his dwelling, pulling up his Character Sheet as he did.

Name: Cash Stone	Class: Cyberknight Level: 30	Experience Points XP 2000000 (2500000)	Hit Points HP 650 (50) (30 per minute)	Stamina ST 650 (30 per minute)	Mana Points MP 525 (25 per minute)
Strength	Constitution	Agility	Dexterity	Mind	Charism

CRAIG ZERF

31	30	31	7	36	a 10
System Points 202				**Credits** 120000	
Weapons – Elemental Ax – Level 7 Cybernetic crossbow – Level 7					
Perks - Personal cybernetic enhancements – Level 7 Cybernetic Armor – Level 7					
Titles – Ursine Exterminator Eager Beaver Lord Appalachia Giant Killer					
Spells – Lightning Bolt – Level 8 Healing – 4 Teleport - 2					
Companions – Bonny Stone Boss Hunter **Level:** 12	**Hit Points** HP 480 (14 per Minute)	**Strength** 19		**Constitution** 19	**Agility** 18	**Mind** 7

CHAPTER 17

Carl Mason stretched his aching back and shook his head. How had things got so fucked up so quickly?

Only ten days ago, the town of Honeydew had been a burgeoning community. High, strong stone walls to keep the monsters at bay. Over four hundred inhabitants. Mana driven power, clean water and ample food.

Then earl Bartholomew Peterson had died. Killed by some monstrosity that the bastard System had called into being.

A terrifying Boss Mob. A Mutant Swamp-demon. A combination of mud and flesh with glowing eyes and ten-foot-long horns. An unstoppable force of evil.

Carl's Identify hadn't been high enough to see its stats, but Bart had told him it was level 25, and an HP of 250.

The Boss had smashed through the town gate and even though they had thrown everything they had at it; they were as chaff in the wind. The highest-level person in the town was Bart, at level 15, followed by Carl at level 12. All the other combatants were between levels 4 and 7.

But what they lacked in levels they made up for with sheer bravery and determination.

And eventually they had taken the boss down. Carl had jumped 2 levels to 14. But they had lost over sixty people. And the worst of it was the loss of their Earl and liege-lord, Bart Peterson.

And with the liege-lord gone, the System no longer recognized his vassals, and as such the town of Honeydew was very swiftly falling apart. The walls were crumbling, the mana-power had ceased, and although there was still access to water, Carl knew it was only a matter of time before that went as well.

To make matters worse, they were being constantly attacked by waves of low-level mobs. Carl wished there was a way he could assume the role of liege-lord, but there was simply no way he could. In fact, he had no idea what to do next. It seemed that the only choices they had were fight and die … or simply give up and die. They couldn't even make a run for it, because once they were outside the crumbling walls, the vast herds of monsters would make short work of them.

He looked at the sky and swore.

"Fuck you all, you Overlord pieces of shit. I hope you all rot in hell."

Then he put his helmet on, shouldered his broadsword and readied himself for yet another battle.

One that would most likely be his last.

***

"My lord, one of the scouts has returned," said lieutenant Jack, saluting as he spoke.

"Talk to me, Jack," said Cash.

"He has seen the town you spoke of, some two miles from here. Tall walls, seems to be quite a lot of people."

Cash grinned. "Excellent news."

Jack shook his head.

"What?"

"The scout informed me that although the town is very much like you said, it is in a terrible state of repair. The walls are crumbling, and they are under attack by hundreds of low-level beasts."

"Holy shit, we need to move, lieutenant, forced march, let's go help these people as soon as."

"Yes. Sir," snapped Jack as he spun around and relayed Cash's orders.

Pre-RPG apocalypse, it would have taken a normal soldier around 25 to 30 minutes to march two miles through thick forest. Special forces could probably do it in under 25 minutes.

But now, even the lowest level Peacekeeper was at least twice as fast and as fit as a top Olympic athlete.

The squad made the forced march in just over five minutes. A feat that would have been considered utterly impossible before.

"Peacekeepers, link shields," commanded Jack.

"Advance towards the city gates. Arbalists, fire at will, concentrate on any mobs closest to the wall. Lady Sarah, any ranged attacks would be appreciated."

"What do you want me and Bonny to do?" asked Cash, giving the lead to his lieutenant to keep a structured chain of command.

"My lord, do what you're best at."

"Get in close and fuck shit up," said Cash with a devilish grin.

"You said it, sir," concurred Jack.

The Peacekeepers moved forward as one, their shields interlocked, forming an impenetrable barrier against the onslaught of low-level mobs. Crossbow bolts flew through the air, finding their mark with deadly accuracy, thinning the ranks of the approaching horde. Sarah, her eyes ablaze with magical power, unleashed a torrent of fireballs that exploded upon impact, incinerating several of the mindless beasts.

Cash, driven by a mix of fury and determination, waded into the fray with a single-minded purpose. His ax cleaved through the air, cutting down mob after mob with lethal precision. The strength and agility bestowed upon him by the System were evident as he moved with a grace and speed that surpassed even the most seasoned warriors.

And next to him, Bonny spun and darted in and out, her powerful jaws tearing and rending her opponents.

The monsters, once a terror to the beleaguered town of Honeydew, now quivered before Cash and his squad's might. He became a whirlwind of death and destruction, his every strike dealing devastating blows.

The battle raged on, the clash of steel against chitinous armor and the roar of the beasts filling the air. The Peacekeepers fought valiantly, their teamwork and training evident in every coordinated strike. They were like a well-oiled death-dealing machine, their movements honed to perfection through many battles.

But amidst the chaos, Cash's mind was singularly focused. He fought not for glory or personal gain, but for the people of Honeydew. Each life lost, each innocent soul taken, fueled his determination to rid the town of the relentless assault.

As the battle raged, the crumbling walls of Honeydew stood as a stark reminder of the desperate situation. Cash knew that time was of the essence. With every swing of his ax, he pushed himself to the limit, his muscles screaming in protest, his body battered and bruised. But he pressed on, knowing that the fate of the town rested on his shoulders.

CHAPTER 18

Carl Mason stood atop the crumbling walls of Honeydew, his eyes wide with awe and disbelief. The sight before him was nothing short of breathtaking, a spectacle that both thrilled and terrified him to the core.

The arrival of Cash Stone and his Peacekeepers had been nothing short of miraculous. Their speed, their strength, their raw and savage power left Carl speechless. He watched in awe as the man who seemed to be mechanically augmented in some way, moved with a grace and speed that defied human capabilities, his ax cleaving through the hordes of low-level mobs with ruthless efficiency. The Peacekeepers fought with a coordinated precision that was both terrifying and mesmerizing to behold.

But it was the magic that truly left Carl dumbfounded. Standing tall, a woman of undeniable beauty, wielded flames that danced with an otherworldly intensity. Fireballs erupted from her hands, engulfing the enemies in a raging inferno. The sheer destructive force of her spells was a sight to behold, leaving Carl in a mix of fear and admiration.

The shield wall, a wall of impenetrable defense, moved with an almost supernatural unity. The soldiers, their shields interlocked, advanced as one, their disciplined movements a testament to their training and skill. Crossbow bolts flew through the air, finding their marks with deadly accuracy. Carl couldn't help but shudder at the sheer efficiency of it all.

As the battle raged on, Carl's heart swelled with relief. The people of Honeydew, his people, were being saved. The thought of their lives hanging in the balance had weighed heavily on his shoulders, but now, seeing these people in action, Carl felt a glimmer of hope ignite within him.

Yet, amidst the relief, a nagging fear lingered in Carl's mind. Could these new arrivals be trusted? Could they truly be the salvation they appeared to be, or were they just another faction seeking to exert control over the people of Honeydew? Carl couldn't shake the sense of unease that gnawed at him, even as he watched Cash's display of power.

The thought of surrendering to this new force, of becoming their prisoners or worse, sent shivers down Carl's spine. He had seen too much bloodshed, too much pain, to simply place blind trust in strangers. But as he watched the cybernetic man fight, saw the determination etched upon his face, Carl couldn't help but hope that maybe, just maybe, they were here to bring salvation.

As the battle reached its climax and the horde of mobs dwindled, Carl felt a mixture of awe, relief, and lingering doubt. The surviving townsfolk emerged from their hiding places, their faces filled with a mix of gratitude and uncertainty. They cheered for Cash and his men, their voices filled with a desperate hope for a brighter future.

Carl descended from the walls, his legs trembling with fatigue. He made his way through the crowd, his eyes fixed on the warrior with the ax. There was something about the man, something that inspired both fear and admiration. Carl couldn't help but wonder what lay beneath that stoic exterior, what dreams and motivations drove him forward.

As Carl reached his side, he found himself standing before the man who had become the town's beacon of hope. He extended a hand, his voice filled with a mixture of gratitude and cautious optimism.

"Thank you, sir. Thank you for saving us," Carl said, his words tinged with a hint of uncertainty.

Cash clasped Carl's hand firmly, his grip strong and reassuring. "Name is Cash Stone. Sorry we didn't get here sooner, but truth be told, I only just heard about you guys."

Carl nodded, a flicker of trust beginning to blossom within him. Perhaps there was hope yet, a glimmer of light in the darkness. The road ahead was uncertain, and the fear lingered, but for now, in this moment, Carl allowed himself to believe that they had found their salvation in the form of Cash Stone and his Peacekeepers.

As the people of Honeydew celebrated their newfound deliverance, Carl couldn't help but cast a wary eye towards their rescuers. The raw and savage power they possessed was undeniable, but only time would tell if they were truly the heroes they appeared to be. For now, Carl would embrace the relief that flooded his heart, holding onto a fragile hope that they had found allies in this treacherous world.

And so, with a mix of awe, gratitude, and lingering doubt, Carl Mason stood amidst the jubilant crowd, his eyes fixed on Cash Stone, the man who had defied all expectations and brought hope to a town on the brink of despair.

CHAPTER 19

"Higgins, why can't I turn Honeydew into a capital city as well?" Cash asked his ever-present AI assistant.

"No dungeon, sir."

"But since we cleared the dungeon under Tomahawk, it's basically just been dormant. So, I don't get it."

"Nothing to get, sir. It's the rules. And as I explained before, a dungeon shouldn't even exist at this stage of the RPG integration. It was a serious anomaly. That is why Tomahawk is the only registered capital city in the System at the moment."

"And if it isn't a capital city, then no shop," noted Cash.

"That is correct, sir," confirmed Higgins. "However, you can still raise a primary residence, a crafting hall, military barracks and so forth."

"But no System Shop."

"A shop is not the be all and end all, sir. If people need anything from the shop, they can always travel to Tomahawk. And after the

Integration, the rules will most likely change, System Shops will be easier to install."

"Well, I need to make a decision. To upgrade and repair Honeydew. Just dump the place and see if the citizens want to take the oath and move to Tomahawk, or just cut and run. Leave them all to their own devices. But that would make me no better than the douchebag Overlords, so probably not that last scenario."

"Why don't you put it to a vote?" asked Sarah. "Give the people some sort of say in their future."

"Because the people generally suck," said Cash. "Trust me, it'll be the usual, I don't take oaths, I don't wanna be a slave, why do you want to be the King of everyone, blah blah fuck you too. And there'll be a bunch who just wanna be in charge, and none of them will appreciate that I'm spending my own hard-earned System points."

"Not necessarily," argued Sarah. "These people are so grateful that we saved them, I'm sure they will be reasonable. Especially Carl who seems like a nice guy."

"Yeah, sure," scoffed Cash. "They were all thankful and full of praise in the aftermath of the battle. Escaping certain death does that, but mark my words, there will be a substantial number of ungrateful asswipes."

"So what? You just gonna dictate to them? Like some sorta tyrant?"

Cash shook his head. "No, I'll call a town meeting and put their choices to them. You're right, there are a lot of good people here. Sometimes I just need to vent, and what are friends for but to have someone to whine too?"

It took almost an hour to collect a quorum of townsfolk together. Cash had asked for a small group of representatives, but Carl had insisted that everyone be present, and eventually it ended up where most of the town was there. Massed in front of the old, crumbling town hall.

Cash stood at the top of the steps, next to him, Carl Mason introduced Cash, even though they all already knew who he was.

Then Cash stepped forward and gave them his pitch.

"Guys," he started, not being one for flowery speeches. "I have a few proposals for you all. Now that the town of Honeydew is temporarily safe, we have some decisions to make before the next lot of beasts attack…"

"What makes you so sure there will be more attacks?" yelled one of the people.

Cash glared at them. "Dude," he said. "Shut up, okay. I'm talking, you can have your say afterwards. Now, as I was saying before this guy opened his yap-hole. I am the liege-lord of Tomahawk, a capital city. In fact, the only capital city currently registered on the system. I am also liege-lord of two more smaller towns, Peach Hamlet and Redwood. Like Honeydew was before, all of those towns have been substantially upgraded. Walls, weapons, water, mana-power, accommodation and more. So, first choice, I can offer you a place to stay in Tomahawk. Housing, food, even a school. There's a lot of opportunity, and if you want you can even take a look at the other two towns, although to be honest, I haven't visited them for a while. You all got that?"

There was a chorus of agreement.

"Fine, secondly, I can upgrade Honeydew, repair it to the state it was before, maybe even make it better. Then you get to stay here, I appoint a leader, or senior advisor and all of us live happily ever after. The final choice, you guys tell me and mine to fuck off, and we comply. Obviously, no one wants that. So, your choice. Make your minds up, but do it quickly, I got time restraints."

The man who had spoken before put his hand up. "Will we have to take a vassal oath to you?"

Cash nodded. "Yep, them's the rules. But you already been through that with your last Liegelord, so you know the drill."

"What if we're not happy with that?"

Cash shrugged. "Not my problem. This isn't about feeling warm and fuzzy, this is about survival. It's about not becoming dead. So, suck it up."

"I advocate we swear the oath to Lord Appalachia," interjected Carl. "I have not known him long, but he seems to be a fair and just man. His squad and he put their lives at risk to help us, and now he is offering to use his own System points to upgrade our town. I feel that we should take his more than generous offer, stay here in Honeydew and do our very best to become a proud part of Lord Appalachia's territory. This is a no-brainer. I'm in."

There was a loud cheer of approval.

"Okay, cool," said Cash. "It looks like the majority are generally happy with staying here and getting a few upgrades. Fine, let's do it."

The oath flashed up on everyone's HUDs and they duly mumbled their way through it.

Afterwards, Cash took his oath to provide and protect.

There was a cacophony of sound, followed by a deluge of colored lights and firework-like explosions.

Congratulations, Lord Appalachia has taken control of the town of Honeydew.

Long may his vassals prosper.
Happy days and much jubilation.

Please be aware that another wave of beasts will soon be attacking the town.
Countdown - seven hours and fifty-nine minutes.
Looks like there's a downside to everything. Sorry about that.

"Fucking bouquet of dicks," muttered Cash.

"Sir, may I bring your attention to the fact that sixteen people have not taken the oath."

Cash glanced at Sarah. "Told you," he said wearily. "There's always gotta be a certain percentage of fucking idiots. Okay, Higgins, point them out."

Not surprisingly, the leader of the holdouts was the man who had been questioning Cash before. And he still had things to say.

"Before we take the oath, I want to know who is going to be in charge, and I would like you to know that before the apocalypse, I was in upper middle management so I feel I am uniquely suited for leadership."

Cash raised an eyebrow. "Carl is senior advisor, and he will select his team."

"And what will my position be? And those of my followers?"

"Followers?" Cash scoffed. "What are you, some sort of prophet. Fuck off, you take the oath or you're banished. I'm not here to negotiate with dickheads. You got seven seconds."

Two of the holdouts stepped forward. "We'll swear."

They duly did so.

"Three seconds left," warned Cash.

"Stop, we need to discuss this," the chief holdout yelled.

"Time up, you're all banished. Now fuck off."

There was an explosion of sound, light, and smoke. And when it cleared, the holdouts were no longer there.

Cash sighed. "I wonder where those assholes go."

"Somewhere else, sir," answered Higgins.

Cash chuckled. "As good an answer as any. Okay, let's kick this pig. Time to get some upgrades. Higgins, put my list up, thanks."

Cash's eyes went blank as he assumed the thousand-yard stare that always accompanied his upgrade perusals.

"Hey, Higgins," he called out, the excitement evident in his voice. "I got a whole new section here. Apparently when you get over five hundred vassals it opens another section. This is awesome."

Cash ran through the list, adding higher walls, watch towers, onagers, a moat, a crafting hall, new accommodation in rows of rooms with shared cooking and ablution areas.

Then he tacked on a meeting hall and a special residence for Carl and another five advisors. Finally, Cash added a small Adventurers guildhall, and a barracks with training area.

Hitting the go button he stood back and watched in wonder as the System did his bidding.

Waves of cheering broke out, some of the townsfolk started dancing, others were so overcome with emotion they burst into tears. Bonny, sensing the excitement, ran around in circles, barking joyfully and licking anyone who came close.

Sarah walked up and placed her hand on Cash's shoulder, giving him an affectionate squeeze. "You done good, lord fancy-pants."

"Yeah," agreed Cash, putting on a supercilious expression. "I am the man."

"Well, you're definitely a man," conceded Sarah. "And I suppose that'll have to do for now."

Carl took a knee before Cash. "My sincere thanks, my lord," he said. His eyes wet with unshed tears.

"No worries, Carl. By the way, I have officially designated you the senior advisor of Honeydew. At the moment, that's the highest rank I can bestow. See that house over there?" Cash pointed a large three-story residence with a hedge and a water fountain outside it. "That's yours. It's also for another five advisers under you. I don't know anyone here, so I'm gonna leave those dudes up to you. Whoever you choose is good by me."

"My lord," acknowledged Carl.

"Now for the really fun part," added Cash as he turned to Sarah and Lieutenant Jack. "Guess what?"

"No," said Sarah. "Not playing silly games. Just tell us."

"The System has added the ability to link all of my towns with gravel roads," stated Cash. "Cool, hey? Proper roads so travel between towns will be easy. Well, easier than trudging through the forest. Plus, the roads come with outposts. Small forts every three miles. They have their own water, mana power, walls and onagers. Brilliant."

"Cost?" asked Sarah.

Cash frowned. "Damned expansive," he admitted. "But I got a shit-house full of System points for this place, plus more for getting over five hundred vassals, so I can afford it. I won't have much left, but that's a problem for another day."

"Go for it," said Sarah.

"Higgins?"

"The Roman Empire put great store in having a decent road system, sir. And they did quite well for themselves."

"Jack?"

"Not for me to say, my lord. But with roads we can look at getting some horses, maybe carts, wagons and such. It would help trade and military. If it were me, I wouldn't hesitate."

Cash pulled up the option on his HUD and hit go.

This time there wasn't the usual razzamatazz involving lights and fanfares. Instead, a solemn note echoed across the land, and a sonorous voice announced.

Hear ye. Hear ye.

Lord Appalachia has just created the first System recognized Territory.

As such, he has been promoted to...
Duke Appalachia.

Let all who serve him praise his name.

Unlike the usual announcements, this one had no sign of snark or sarcasm. In fact, it sounded downright respectful.

"Holy fuck, those bastards," grunted Cash.

"How could they?"

"What?" asked Sarah, worried that something terrible may have happened.

"They just tacked another 5 points onto my Charisma," sighed Cash. "At 15 points, I am now officially the fucking prom king."

CHAPTER 20

The air crackled with anticipation as Cash Stone stood atop the newly fortified walls of Honeydew, his eyes scanning the horizon for any sign of movement.

"My friends," he bellowed with a voice like thunder. "Today we face our first test! Are we prepared to protect all we have built here?" The townsfolk, armed and ready, roared in response, their hearts pounding in their chests. They had witnessed the transformation of their humble town into a formidable fortress, and now they were about to put its strength to the ultimate test.

"Oooh, look at you with you massively inflated Charisma stats. Soon you'll be competing for America Idol."

"Fuck off," grunted Cash.

Sarah chuckled.

The countdown hit zero, and the sky lit up with a flash of pale blue light. A low rumble built as an army of monsters surged through the surrounding forest, blanketing Honeydew in an oppressive wave of squeals and growls. Dozens of creatures leapt from the ground and the branches, their eyes glowing red with malice. The townsfolk braced themselves for the onslaught.

Cash Stone equipped his ax, and the metal glinted in the flickering light of the surrounding flames. He looked to his right and left, meeting the eyes of his fellow fighters, all of them ready to spill their blood for the town they loved.

The first wave crashed against the walls, and the townsfolk fought back with all their might. The sound of steel clashing against scales echoed through the night air, and the smell of blood mixed with the scent of burning wood. Sarah stood by Cash's side, a fireball ready in her hand, her eyes scanning the battlefield for any sign of weakness in their defenses.

From the vantage point of a parapet on the town walls, Cash observed with keen interest as the citizens of Honeydew sprang into action. Carl, now a Senior Advisor and in charge of the town's defenses and strategy, barked orders with a commanding voice, rallying his team. Under Carl's direction, crossbowmen strung their bows and aimed at distant enemies. As one they fired, their bolts whistling through the air and finding their mark in the chests of charging beasts.

But it was the onagers that stole the show. These massive war machines, crafted with meticulous care and powered by the newly restored mana reserves, unleashed devastating salvos of destruction. Rocks and projectiles soared through the air, obliterating their targets with bone-crushing force. The ground shook as the monstrous beasts were sent flying, their bodies torn apart in a spectacular display of power.

Cash couldn't help but smile as he witnessed the havoc wreaked by the onagers. Their installation had been a stroke of genius, and the townsfolk marveled at the destruction they wrought. The beasts that managed to breach the walls were met with a wall of shields and swords, the citizens fighting with a newfound ferocity and skill.

Cash watched as the townspeople of Honeydew ferociously battled their attackers, every swing of their weapons gleaming in the torchlight. As one fell to the ground, another stepped forward, taking up his fallen comrade's weapon and continuing the fight. In that moment, Cash felt a deep sense of pride for his fellow citizens. They fought with purpose, every movement deliberate and calculated. Their dedication radiated from them like a tangible force. It was clear they would not let their home fall to destruction.

Carl, his face streaked with dirt and sweat, approached Cash, a triumphant gleam in his eyes. "We did it, my lord," he exclaimed, the joy evident in his voice. "The town held, and we've pushed the beasts back."

Cash grunted, feigning his usual grumpy

demeanor. "Don't get too cocky," he replied, a smirk tugging at the corners of his mouth. "We've only just begun. There will be more battles to come."

The citizens of Honeydew erupted into cheers, their voices filling the air with a resounding roar of victory. Morale was high, and a newfound sense of camaraderie filled the town. Cash had become a symbol of hope, a leader they could rally behind.

As the cheers subsided, Cash addressed the crowd, his voice carrying over the din. "This victory belongs to all of you," he declared. "Together, we have shown the beasts that we will not be conquered. Honeydew will stand strong, and we will protect our home at all costs."

The citizens cheered once more, their adulation washing over Cash like a wave of warmth. Deep down, he felt a sense of satisfaction and accomplishment. Despite his gruff exterior, he cherished the admiration of the townsfolk. They had become his family, and their unwavering support fueled his determination to protect them.

The battle had been won, but the war was far from over. Cash knew that there were more survivors out there, more towns in need of their help. With Honeydew fortified and united, they were now ready to venture forth, to extend their protection to those who still fought for survival.

But for now, they would revel in their victory, savoring the moment of triumph. The town of Honeydew had proven its resilience, and Cash had cemented his place as their champion. As he looked out over the cheering crowd, he couldn't help but feel a surge of optimism. Together, they would face whatever challenges awaited them, armed with the strength of their unity and the unyielding spirit that burned within them.

CHAPTER 21

Cash stood on the walls of Tomahawk, his gaze fixed on the newly constructed gravel roads that stretched into the distance. The townsfolk buzzed with excitement as they marveled at the prospect of connecting their town to the neighboring settlements. The roads held the promise of trade, communication, and a newfound sense of unity.

But Cash had something else in mind.

He turned to Gunny, and spoke with a determined tone. "Gunny, we need to form a cavalry section. With these new roads, we can harness the power of mounted troops to enhance our capabilities. I want to concentrate on cavalry."

Gunny nodded, a glint of excitement in his eyes. "A cavalry section, sir? That's a bold move, but it could give us a decisive advantage."

"Yep, look I know a bit about horses and riding, but I'm no cowboy. You got any ideas on someone, or even a few someone's who could run with this idea?"

"Off the top of my head, yeah," answered

Gunny. "Two of my men used to be day workers. Went from ranch to ranch around here. I'm sure they would be happy to get involved."

"Go get them," said Cash.

As Gunny set off, Cash's mind wandered to his own past. Before the world changed, he had been an avid horseback rider, finding solace and freedom in the saddle. The memories of those carefree days stirred something within him. A longing to reclaim a piece of his former life that was a part of him before those assholes took his legs.

He turned to Sarah, who had just climbed the stairs to join him on the wall. "I told Gunny about the cavalry idea. He's off to fetch a couple of cowboys. Hey, did I ever tell you that I used to be quite the rider before I lost my legs?" he asked with a wistful smile.

Sarah's eyes widened in surprise. "No, Cash, you never mentioned it. I can't imagine you on a horse."

Cash chuckled. "Well, it's been a while, but I reckon I still have some riding skills buried deep down. Actually, there used to be a company that organized trail riding outings nearby, and there's a ranch a few miles away. Called Arrowmount. We should scout the area, see if any horses have survived and can be rounded up."

The sound of Gunny returning drew Cash's attention. The former Marine entered, behind him were two men Cash hadn't met before. They were both of a type. Five ten, rangy, clear-eyed, unshaven. Both wore Stetsons.

They nodded to Cash as Gunny introduced them.

"Jeb, and Caleb."

"My lord," they replied in unison.

"Gunny told you my idea?"

"Sure did," said Caleb. "It makes sense. But I can't say I seen many horses around. Most likely the monsters ate them all up. Hard for a horse to fight a mutant wolf or such."

"Dunno about that," interjected Jeb. "I seen myself some ornery stallions. Seen one kick a coyote to death once."

Caleb shrugged. "Just saying, ain't seen no horses."

"I was saying to lady Sarah, there was a company that did trail riding nearby, and there's a ranch a few miles away. Called Arrowmount. We could start there."

Caleb shook his head. "Trail riders got crap horses. Arrowmount, that used to be Alex Sumner's place. Good horses. Also, Two Rocks, other side of Arrowmount, plus Double Diamond. We need a few more people who know at least a bit about horses. They don't need to be no wranglers or nothing. Even Sunday riders will do. Long as they don't crap their jeans at the sight of a horse."

"I reckon you get Greta to put out a general notice," suggested Gunny. "This won't be restricted to the Peacemakers."

"I agree," confirmed Cash. "Let's get right on to that. Could you two put together a list of what we might need. Give it to lady Sarah. Let's move it, time is wasting."

***

As the sun rose on a new day, Cash looked back at the team he had put together.

He had put Jeb and Caleb in charge of all things horse. They had interviewed a few people and ended up with a group of seven they considered not too crap, as Jeb put it. Then they had scoured the city for all and any riding equipment they could find. Saddles, reins, bridles, anything at all. Then they had added oats, carrots, apples and sugar lumps.

The team had loaded all of the kit into their Inventories, and now they were setting off towards Arrowmount. Cash pushed the team hard, a fast jog with Bonny scouting out in front. Cash could have quintupled his speed with ease, but he was many Levels above everyone else, so he had to keep their progress down to the slowest amongst them.

But still, they were traveling at least three times faster than pre-apocalyptic humans could have. Cash also noticed that they were not being overly accosted by any mobs. When he brought that fact up with Higgins, his assistant had explained that lower-level mobs could sense Cash's inordinately high levels, and as such, only the most aggressive, or suicidal of them would attack.

After a couple of hours of hard humping, Caleb pulled up next to Cash and Sarah.

"I reckon we getting close to Arrowmount," he said. "Hard to tell with the Overlords fucking the place up so much, but I got a feeling like this is the ranch."

Cash called Bonny over. "We looking for a ranch," he told her. "With horses." As he spoke, Cash tried to project the image of a horse into Bonny's mind. The massive Tamaskan cocked her head to one side and nodded.

"You think she gets it?" asked Caleb.

"Sure," answered Cash. "Well, I hope so. Let's see."

Ten minutes later Bonny returned, barked once and took off again.

The team followed close behind.

Finally, they arrived at the ranch. Or at least what was left of it.

The once bustling establishment lay in ruins, its stables dilapidated and overgrown with weeds. The horses were long gone, but hope flickered in Cash's eyes. "Let's search the surrounding area," he suggested. "The horses might have roamed free and found shelter elsewhere."

They ventured deeper into the forest, but as they came across the remains of barns, paddocks and accommodation, it became apparent that the ranch had suffered some form of monster attack. The place had been utterly destroyed.

"Bonny, can you smell any horses?" asked Cash.

Bonny shook her head and gave her companion a sad look. On the other hand, dogs tend to specialize in sad looks, but it was plain that the horses hadn't survived whatever had happened to the place.

"Double Diamond next," said Jeb as he led the way.

Twenty minutes later, Bonny came sprinting back towards them, her tongue lolling out and a large doggy grin on her face. Cash got the distinct impression of a herd of horse in his mind as she approached. He threw his arms around Bonny as she got close to him.

"Clever girl," he praised. "You found some horses."

Bonny nodded.

"Take us to them," Cash told her.

Ten minutes later, the team were crouched down behind whatever cover they could find.

"Holy crap," breathed Jeb. "What the fuck happened to those horses?"

"They look okay," said Cash. "I mean, maybe a bit more muscular than I remember, but nice and healthy."

"A bit more muscular? My lord," continued Jeb. "Those fuckers are like the Rock of horseflesh. It's like they bin jacked up on steroids. Also, maybe you can't tell because of perspective, but I bin lookin' at horses my whole life, so I can tell. Those SOB's are like 25 to 30 hands high."

"Okay, let's assume I have no idea what that means," said Cash. "Explain."

"A normal pony is maybe 14 to 16 hands. A big fucker is around 20. These guys are the equivalent of a man who stands eight to nine feet tall and weighs in at over four hundred pounds."

"That's a big man," quipped Cash. "And those are big horses. Higgins, how they get so humongous?"

Before Higgins could answer, there was a disturbance in the surrounding forest and a pack of six or seven large wolves came running out. Their fur gleamed like metal, and their teeth were obviously also System enhanced in some way. But instead of the herd of horses acting in any way panicked, the head stallion turned towards the incoming wolves and attacked, followed by at least ten other herd members.

And what should have been a one-sided fight that favored the iron-wolves ended up being totally the opposite. The mega-horses simply tore the wolves apart with teeth, and hooves.

The team watched in amazement as the horses fought as a unit, spinning and charging and trampling. Finally, the last two wolves turned and fled.

"Well, I'll be," grunted Caleb. "I told you horses could be ornery. Now you all know what I meant."

"And I believe that answers your prior question, sir," added Higgins. "The horses have obviously been gaining levels by slaughtering any predators that have attempted to eat them. What you now have are a herd of super-horses."

"That," said Cash with a grin. "Is awesome. Jeb, Caleb, you reckon we could still ride them?"

"Don't see why not," answered Caleb. "A horse is a horse, I'm sure they still think the same. Here," he pulled a few apples out of his Inventory, kept some and handed a couple to Jeb. "The two of us will go have a chat to them. See what happens."

The rest of the team watched with bated breath, except for Bonny who seemed to be remarkably chilled.

Cash scratched her ears and she looked up at him, projecting a vision of Cash riding the massive black stallion. "Really, my girl," said Cash, his voice slightly amused. "You reckon that big musclebound horsey will let me on its back?"

Bonny nodded.

Cash looked up to see both Caleb and Jeb standing calmly in front of the black stallion. They held out the apples, their palms flat, and the massive horse delicately took them and crunched them with obvious relish. When the stallion had finished the apples on offer, Cash walked forward.

The stallion stepped up and then, after staring at Cash for a few second, it bent its forelegs and sank to its knees.

Cash put his hand out and rubbed the huge horse's neck. The stallion responded with a low whinny and pushed its nose against Cash.

"I have no idea what's going on here," said Jeb

quietly. "But I ain't never seen the like."

Without any further thought, Cash leaped onto the stallion's back and the giant horse immediately started to run. Bonny ran with them, tongue lolling, an expression of contentment on her doggy face.

"Well, shit," said Caleb as he watched Cash disappear into the forest. "Ain't that one for the books. I do surely hope that stallion don't kill the boss. Because that would surely put a black mark on the day."

CHAPTER 22

"You can't call a magnificent beast like that, Stanley," scoffed Sarah.

"Can. In fact, I just did," stated Cash.

"Storm, or Tornado or Styx," continued Sarah. "Awe inspiring names. Not fucking Stanley."

"I had an uncle, Stanley," said Cash. "Loved him. He used to dress up as Santa Claus."

"Just because an uncle used to dress up on Christmas day, doesn't mean you should name the world's most impressive stallion after him."

"No, not just Christmas day," said Cash. "Always. He always dressed like Santa Claus. Used to make us sit on his lap. Actually, now I think about it, uncle Stanley was a bit of a perv. Still, that's his name. Discussion over. I'm the fucking king around here, and what I say goes."

"King, shming," grunted Sarah.

"Lord then, whatever. What you calling your mount?"

Sarah looked over at the beautiful honey colored Palomino and smiled. "Cisco."

Cash nodded. "Good name," he admitted. "I

mean, it's no Stanley, but it'll do."

Cash scoped the herd from atop his horse. All around him there were about fifty animals, their coats blending black, chestnut and grey in the morning light. He could make out two proud stallions, a few ponies and colts, as well as four mares heavy with foal. Jeb rode up alongside him, telling him they'd be due in the next couple of weeks. Cash nodded, happy the herd would be getting even bigger soon.

Gunny brought Jeb and Caleb under the auspices of the Peacekeepers and gave them both the rank of lieutenant. Then the two cowboys put together a team of thirty to start with. Twenty riders, and ten for logistics, stabling, taking care of the tack, feeding and such what. The twenty riders were further broken down into two squads of ten, one under each lieutenant.

Cash spent some credits at the System Shop and bought enough kit to supply each rider with a cavalry sword, armor, a small crossbow and a light lance. The riders practiced mounted archery for two weeks until their crossbows felt like an extension of both hands.

Jeb and Caleb peered suspiciously at the new cavalry, their faces grim. Despite their misgivings, Cash declared he was taking one of the squads with him, and without hesitation chose Jeb's team —not because they were superior, but merely because Jeb had been standing next to him when he made the declaration. The sun had yet to rise when they left early the following morning.

Cash planned on visiting Peach Hamlet and Redwood. He felt genuinely guilty that he basically owned both of those towns and had never returned to either of them since they had sworn vassalage to him. But in fairness, he had been busy. Now with the new roads and the horses, he had no excuse.

Two days later they were approaching the town of Peach Hamlet, Bonny was roving ahead as usual, and the rest of the squad was riding two abreast when the walls came into view.

As they approached a trio of guards popped up on the wall next to the closed gate and trained their crossbows in the squad.

"Halt," shouted the one. "Who goes there?"

"It's me," yelled Cash.

"No shit. Look, I have no idea who you are, but we don't do strangers here. Turn around and go back whence you came."

"Or what?" asked Cash.

"Or we'll turn you all into pincushions."

"Stop being a dick. Look, I'll give you the benefit of the doubt here. Do yourself a favor and go fetch Father O'Reilly."

"No need," stated the guard. "I'm the senior watch commander. What I say goes. Don't need no Paladin to tell me what to do."

"Listen up, ex-senior watch commander…"

"What you mean, ex?"

"You just been fired."

"By who's authority?" laughed the guard.

"Mine. Lord Appalachia. Now open the fucking gates before I strike you down, tear your head off and piss down your neck."

The guard flinched. "Bullshit. Lord Appalachia's a myth."

One of the other guards leaned closer to the ex-watch commander and said something in his ear.

"Really?" responded the ex.

The guard nodded.

"Hold up your left hand," requested the ex.

Cash grinned as he held up his cybernetic limb.

"Oh, crap," grunted the ex-watch commander. He turned to the guard who had just spoken to him. "Run, get the Father. Now."

Less than two minutes later the gates began to grind open.

Cash nudged Stanley forward and the rest of the squad followed.

Father O'Reilly was standing just inside the gate to welcome them. As was the ex-watch commander, who was on his knees next to the Paladin.

"Welcome, lord Appalachia," greeted O'Reilly. "I believe you have just demoted our watch commander. May I ask for some clemency on his behalf?"

"How's it hanging, Father," returned Cash. "In answer to your question, no. The guy's a professional dickhead."

"In all fairness, my lord, he had no idea who

you were."

"That makes it even worse," snapped Cash. "In this fucked up new world, every survivor is precious. Every human life, sacrosanct. But instead of welcoming us, or even bothering to find out who we were, fuckwit here decided to belittle and threaten us. I'm in a mind to banish him, let alone not show him any leniency whatsoever." Cash turned to Sarah and shook his head. "Sometimes I hate being right," he continued. "But what do I always say?"

"There's always at least one complete dickhead," answered Sarah.

"What's your name?" Cash asked the disgraced guard.

"Thomas, my lord."

"Thomas, do you understand what I just said? You know, about people being precious and about you being a self-important piece of offal?"

"Yes, my lord."

"And what have you got to say for yourself? And think before you answer, I don't want some rote crap about being sorry. I need some honesty here, if you're capable of it."

Thomas thought for a while, then he spoke, still on his knees, his eyes down. "I thought that by belittling others, I could raise myself. I think that maybe I was acting the big deal because I always felt that others looked down on me. I… I…" Thomas's statement stuttered to an end. "I don't rightly know why I acted like that, my lord," he finished.

Cash dismounted and walked up to the kneeling man. "Stand."

Thomas stood up, eyes downcast, his face etched with obvious fear.

"Look at me," Cash commanded. "Thomas, I can't have people in responsible positions acting like self-important assholes."

Thomas nodded. "I accept whatever punishment you give me, my lord."

"Yeah, buddy, that goes without saying. Tell me, Thomas, were you a good watch commander?"

"I thought so, my lord. I have never turned anyone else away, but that was only because no one else ever showed up."

"He is a brave man," interjected Father O'Reilly. "And his men seem to like him."

"Thomas, I'm going to leave you in charge. You are still the watch commander. But I swear, I hear you backsliding into your dickish ways, I will personally tear you a new one. Understand?"

Thomas dropped to his knees again. "Thank you, my lord, I am your man, for now and forever."

"Yeah, whatever, now fuck off, there's a good chap." Cash turned to the Father as Thomas scuttled off, his face alight with newfound purpose. "So, Father, what's happening?"

"Come, my lord," answered O'Reilly. "Lets us take drink and talk. I feel there is much you need to tell us about. The roads for one."

Cash nodded. "Hey, Jeb, put the horses in the

square, then come find me. I'll be in the big house. Lady Sarah, with me. Okay, Father. Let's go do some talking."

"And drinking," added Sarah.

"You go girl," joshed Cash.

CHAPTER 23

Cash Stone stood at the heart of Peach Hamlet, his gaze fixed on the bustling activity around him. He had just used a pile of his System Points to construct a barracks and a crafting hall that now stood as a testament to their progress, a tangible representation of their collective determination to build a better future. Cash had also sprung for a moat. And that was now filled with shimmering water, adding an additional layer of defense to the growing settlement.

But despite the sense of accomplishment, Cash felt a tinge of melancholy. He had expended his last remaining System points, leaving him devoid of the resource that had propelled his advancements thus far. He turned to Higgins, the ever-present voice of reason and knowledge, seeking guidance.

"Higgins, how can I obtain more System points?" Cash asked, his voice laced with a hint of frustration.

Higgins stroked his chin, his expression thoughtful. "Ah, System points, a bit of a mystery, sir. As far as I can gather, it seems that acquiring more System points involves a combination of fighting Boss mobs, discovering and saving survivors, and expanding your influence by gaining more vassals."

Cash sighed, his shoulders slumping. "So, we'll have to rely on our wits and sheer determination, as always. No easy way out. Plus, I'm feeling a little low on wits right now."

Higgins nodded, a faint smile playing on his lips. "Indeed, sir. But if anyone can find a way, it's you."

Determined to make the most of their current situation, Cash turned his attention to Father O'Reilly, the steadfast paladin in charge of Peach Hamlet. "Father O'Reilly, I'll be heading to Redwood next," he announced, his voice carrying a mix of purpose and anticipation.

Father O'Reilly's brow furrowed, his face etched with concern. "My lord, I must warn you. Our scouts have reported signs of something immense lurking in the forest between Peach Haven and Redwood. While they haven't laid eyes on the creature itself, the hooved tracks they found suggest a massive entity, possibly thirty feet tall and weighing over three tons. It could be a formidable foe."

Cash let out a chuckle, attempting to mask his unease. "Well, Father, for all we know, if it's got hooves, it could just be a really big goat."

Sarah, always quick-witted and ready with a

retort, interjected. "Or a demon, Cash. You know, just to keep things interesting."

Cash shook his head, a mixture of exasperation and amusement evident on his face. "You had to jinx us, didn't you? Now we've got a fucking demon to deal with. Why did you have to say that?"

With their banter lightening the mood, Cash gathered his resolve and addressed the gathered townsfolk. "Fear not, my friends! Whether it be a goat, a demon, or something entirely unexpected, we will face this challenge head-on. Together, we have overcome countless trials, and this will be no different. Redwood awaits, and we shall bring our strength and determination to its doorstep."

The surrounding townsfolk cheered in response, their spirits buoyed by Cash's unwavering resolve. The feeling of unity and camaraderie filled the air, mingling with the anticipation of the impending adventure.

"Oh, well said, sir," encouraged Higgins.

"Yes, very heroic," added Sarah. "Almost Shakesperean. And the people love it."

Cash grimaced. "Fucking high Charisma stat strikes again."

As the preparations for their journey to Redwood commenced, Cash Stone focused his attention on the newly formed cavalry detachment.

Cash approached Jeb, a broad smile on his face. "Jeb, my friend, ready to ride into the unknown?" Jeb grinned back, his eyes gleaming with excitement.

"You know it, my lord. Can't resist the thrill of the open road and the possibility of facing down a massive goat-headed demon. It's what dreams are made of."

Cash chuckled, adjusting the straps on his riding gear. "Ah, the demon talk again. Sarah seems to have everyone convinced we're going to run into some colossal monster. Just our luck, right?"

Sarah, joining the conversation, raised an eyebrow mischievously. "Oh, come on, lord fancy-pants. Where's your sense of adventure? You can't deny that a little demon hunting spices things up."

Cash rolled his eyes playfully. "Spices things up, she says. Well, I hope you're ready to back up your claims with some fireballs, my fiery friend."

Sarah smirked, a glint of determination in her eyes. "You know I'm always ready to unleash some flames. Just make sure you keep up, Cash."

As the banter continued, the cavalry detachment gathered their horses, checking their equipment with practiced precision. The anticipation among the riders was palpable, a blend of excitement and trepidation as they prepared to venture into the unknown.

Cash mounted his horse, his gaze sweeping over the determined faces of his comrades. "Remember, everyone, we're not just out here for a joyride. We're here to scout the area, search for any signs of life or valuable resources, and, of course, round up any surviving horses we come across."

Jeb nodded, a gleam of seriousness replacing his earlier jovial demeanor. "We'll do our best, my lord. You can count on us to ride hard and ride true."

With the detachment assembled, Cash gave a nod of approval. "Alright, my friends, let's show this demon-infested world what we're made of. Forward, to Redwood!"

As they took off, Cash shook his head and mumbled to himself. "What the fuck is wrong with me? I'm starting to talk all weird."

"If I may, sir," interjected Higgins who was currently flowing next to Cash. "As the System nears the point of Integration, the Event Horizon, as it were, many subtle changes will begin to occur."

"Like what?"

"Well, you are already aware of the fact that pre-apocalyptic structures are degrading a lot faster than would naturally happen. Roads, housing, bridges and so forth. The closer we get, the quicker this shall proceed. Soon clothing, steel structures, even much of the pre-RPG flora and fauna shall undergo various changes. On top of this, the System with begin to subtly alter your speech patterns to keep you more in tune with your surrounds. Id Est, you will find yourselves communicating in a style that is more Medieval vernacular than modern American."

"You mean like, thee and thou and good morrow kind sir?"

"Ostensibly, yes. Although most likely not as radical as that."

"So I'm gonna start sounding like some limp-wristed Limey?"

"I find that comment rather offensive, sir," scowled Higgins. "After all, the British did invent the language."

"Fuck that," grunted Cash. "Those Overlord dick-sandwiches ain't gonna make me start talking like a fag."

Higgins shook his head. "How is it possible for a living being with a Charisma stat in double figures to be such an offensive scoundrel?"

"Higgy-baby…"

"Yes, sir. I know – fuck off."

Cash grinned. "You got it."

The cavalry detachment set off, their horses' hooves pounding against the newly laid gravel road. The wind whipped through their hair, carrying a sense of adventure and purpose as they rode toward the forest that held the unknown. As they ventured deeper into the dense woods, Cash couldn't shake the feeling of anticipation tinged with caution. The towering trees seemed to close in around them, casting long shadows on the forest floor. The distant sounds of rustling leaves and the occasional hoot of an owl added an eerie atmosphere to their journey.

The riders pushed on, their horses snorting

with excitement and anticipation. The forest grew darker and more foreboding, the twisted branches above casting a shadowy canopy that hid any potential threats lurking within.

Suddenly, the ground shook beneath their horses' hooves, a rumble reverberating through the air. Ahead, a monstrous figure emerged from the dense foliage. It was the massive goat-headed demon they had anticipated, its towering form casting an imposing silhouette against the dim light.

Jeb's eyes widened, his grip on the reins tightening. "Well, my lord, it seems our demon hunt just got real."

"Thanks, Sarah," yelled Cash. "Now look what you've done."

"That's not how life works. Just by saying something doesn't make it happen."

"Law of attraction," argued Cash. "Or manifestation, or something. Whatever, everyone knows that you can jinx something by talking about it."

"I think you're talking about paranoid schizophrenia," quipped Sarah.

"Hey, just because you might be paranoid, doesn't mean they're not out to get you," said Cash. "Jeb, we don't want to take this massive motherfucker on in the trees. Let's run away for a bit until we find a clearing so we can use our mobility to grind it down."

Cash used Identify, and then almost

immediately wished he hadn't. Sometimes ignorance is bliss. Particularly when it is folly to be wise.

Malignant Caprine (demon goat) – *Level 39*
HP *- 450*
Strength – *Clawed attack, crushing hooves*
Weakness – *Restricted mobility*

Obeying Cash's suggestion, the detachment wheeled away and galloped towards the last clearing they had ridden through.

"Not too fast," yelled Sarah. "We don't want it to lose us."

"No chance of that," said Cash as one of the demon-goat's claws slashed through the air just behind him. "This fucker is faster than shit outa a goose."

Within a few frantic minutes, they made it to the clearing, a large glade with a few short shrubs and a fairly flat surface. Perfect for the horses to maneuver on.

"Wheel back," shouted Jeb. "Close order, level lances. Let's show Billy-goat Gruff how we do things Tomahawk style."

With a shout, the cavalry detachment charged forward, their horses surging with incredible speed. Lances leveled, they aimed for the demon's vulnerable points, their coordination honed through rigorous training.

As they closed in on the demon, the air

crackled with tension. Cash's mana crossbow bolts flew through the air, finding their marks with deadly accuracy. Sarah's fireballs erupted, scorching the demon's hide with searing flames. The demon bellowed in fury, swiping at the riders with its massive claws.

Cash, leading the charge, focused his mind and summoned his lightning-infused powers. Bolts of crackling energy shot from his fingertips, striking the demon's horns and hindering its movements. His attacks were precise and devastating, each strike dealing a massive blow to the beast. But even though Cash was level 30, this monster was almost fifty percent higher than him. Or in technical terms, a shithouse full.

The clash between cavalry and demon created a whirlwind of chaos and bravery. Swords clashed, lances shattered, and the ground trembled with the force of their battle. The riders with their outsized System enhanced horses and their personal strength, fought with a synchronized precision that showcased their training and resilience.

Through the fierce melee, Cash's eyes locked onto the demon's glowing red gaze. He knew that defeating this creature was crucial, not only for their own survival but to inspire hope among the survivors.

With a burst of adrenaline-fueled energy, Cash urged Stanley forward, closing the gap between him and the demon in the blink of an eye. He channeled all his power into a devastating strike. Lightning crackled around him as he swung his ax with a mighty flourish, aiming for the demon's exposed neck.

The blade connected with a resounding impact, slicing through the demon's thick hide. A triumphant roar echoed through the forest as the creature collapsed to the ground.

The rest of the detachment wheeled in unison and savagely attacked the downed demon.

Bonny used the opportunity to clamp her impressive jaws around its neck and whipping back and forth she tore its throat open.

Cheers erupted among the riders, their victory sending ripples of elation through their ranks. Cash, his body trembling with exertion, dismounted and approached the fallen demon. With a final blow, he severed its horns as a trophy, a symbol of their triumph.

As the dust settled and the adrenaline began to subside, Cash felt a surge of energy within him. His body pulsed with power, and a notification appeared before his eyes.

Level Up!

Cash Stone reached level 32, gaining new abilities and an increase in his stats. The battle had not only rewarded him with experience but also bestowed upon him valuable System points that replenished his dwindling supply.

A wide grin spread across his face as he realized the potential that lay before him. With newfound strength and resources, he could continue to build a future for humanity in this war-torn world.

Turning to his comrades, Cash raised his ax high. "We have proven our mettle today, my friends! This victory belongs to all of us. Let it be known that the cavalry of Tomahawk will face any challenge head-on, and emerge victorious!"

The riders cheered, their spirits soaring as they reveled in their triumph. They knew that, with Cash leading the way, there was hope for a brighter future.

As they continued their journey towards Redwood, their hearts were filled with newfound determination. The cavalry detachment, inspired by their recent victory, rode on with a renewed sense of purpose, ready to face whatever challenges lay ahead.

CHAPTER 24

Name: Cash Stone	Class: Cyberknight Level: 32	Experience Points XP 3000000 (3500000)	Hit Points HP 850 (50) (30 per minute)	Stamina ST 850 (30 per minute)	Mana Points MP 600 (25 per minute)
Strength 33	Constitution 32	Agility 31	Dexterity 7	Mind 36	Charisma 16
System Points 127			Credits 120000		
Weapons – Elemental Ax – Level 9 Cybernetic crossbow – Level 8					
Perks - Personal cybernetic enhancements – Level 8 Cybernetic Armor – Level 8					
Titles – Ursine Exterminator Eager Beaver Duke Appalachia Giant Killer					
Spells – Lightning Bolt – Level 9 Healing – 4 Teleport - 2					
Companions – Bonny Stone Boss Hunter Level: 14	Hit Points HP 500 (14 per Minute)	Strength 20	Constitution 19	Agility 19	Mind 7

"Got another point to Charisma," snapped Cash.

"Ooh, I swoon in your very presence, my lord," scoffed Sarah.

"Actually, lady Sarah," interjected Higgins. "Now that mister Stone has been promoted to a Duke, he is no longer a lord. The correct way to address him is, your Grace."

"Seriously?" asked Sarah.

"Indubitably, my lady."

It had only been a few minutes since the detachment had downed the Goat Demon thingy, and as it was a high-level boss, it had given all involved a fair amount of loot, including a small chest for each member of the team.

The cavalry all received upgraded lances. Light, slightly longer than their standard issue, but with a much higher durability and more than double the damage.

Sarah got an upgraded fireball scroll. Bonny received a close-fitting doggy-helmet that allowed her ears to pop out and upgraded her protection stats.

Cash got another power cell for his cybernetic arm.

As well as this they all got the usual skin, flesh, teeth, claws and sundry body parts that could be either sold to the System shop, or to the burgeoning number of new craftsmen in the towns.

"Higgins, when we were fighting the goat-boy, I managed to combine a lightning strike with my ax. It didn't work as well as I would like, but it definitely added some damage."

"Yes, sir," answered Higgins. "If you recall, your ax is able to utilize various powers. Earth, water, lightning and so forth. But as I informed you before, only when you reach a much higher level, and when the ax itself is leveled up."

"What level?" asked Cash.

"Usually, the ax needs to be level 10. I assume

you are getting close and that is why the powers are beginning to manifest. Simply keep at it, your Grace, and practice shall perfection make."

"Yeah, sure," responded Cash. "Jeb, let's saddle up. Head for Redwood."

"Right away, your Grace."

"Really?" sighed Cash.

"Mister Higgins informed us that was the correct form of address," said Jeb.

Cash didn't answer as he climbed into the saddle and they set off.

Two hours later, the walls of Redwood hove into view.

"Place looks pretty much exactly like when I last saw it," said Cash.

"Why wouldn't it?" questioned Sarah.

"Just saying," said Cash.

As they rode closer, he took note of two guards standing on the wall next to the gate.

"Hey," one called out. "Who you guys? And where'd you get such huge horses?"

"Name's Cash Stone. You may have heard of me."

The guard nodded. "Didn't you used to be the Commander or something? We all thought you were dead."

"Not so much," answered Cash.

"And now he's a Duke," interjected Sarah. "So you have to call him, your Grace."

"No shit?" asked the guard, looking suitably impressed. "Hold, your Grace. We'll open the gates for you."

"A better reception than Peach Hamlet," commented Sarah.

"Yeah, a bit too friendly," said Jeb. "Didn't even ask for proof or fetch someone who may have been able to verify you are who you say you are."

Cash shrugged. "True, but I'm just happy that he's not a complete dick."

The gates creaked open and Cash led the way through, Bonny walking at Stanley's side. The Tamaskan was now so large, that even though she was dwarfed by the oversized horse, she was still as big as a decent size pony. Plus the mental images she used to communicate with Cash were getting easier to understand.

As they entered the town of Redwood, Cash couldn't help but notice the signs of neglect. Buildings showed signs of wear and tear, and the streets were in need of repair. The townsfolk moved about with a sense of lethargy, lacking the discipline and vigor that he had come to expect.

A man standing near the entrance, gave Cash a sloppy salute, as did the two guards flanking him.

"Commander," he hailed. "My name is Aidan Barton, I am the duly elected leader of Redwood. Welcome, sir."

"Actually, it's your Grace," interjected Sarah. He's Duke Appalachia now. Keep up, dude."

Aidan flushed with embarrassment. I apologize, your Grace."

Cash surveyed the town with a critical eye.

"Aidan, this place is falling apart. Discipline is lacking, the people look underfed. What happened?"

Aidan sighed, his shoulders slumping. "I did my best, your Grace, but it's been tough. We've had an influx of survivors in the last few months, and it's been a struggle to manage everything. We're low on food, the guards aren't keeping to a proper schedule, and I admit, things have started to slip."

Cash's voice hardened. "Aidan, you need to step up or step aside. You can't let this town crumble under your watch. Either find an efficient assistant who can help you manage the affairs here, or consider resigning."

Aidan's face flushed with embarrassment, but he nodded. "You're right, sir. I've let things slide, and it's time to take responsibility. I'll find someone who can assist me and ensure that Redwood thrives."

"You say you've had survivors arrive, when, how many and where are they from?"

Aidan shrugged. "A few, your Grace. Over time, to tell the truth, I'm not sure where they've all come from. Here and there, I presume."

Cash jumped off Stanley and walked up to Aiden, his expression thunderous. "You have gotta be shitting me," he yelled. "Did you send out scouts to look for more of them? Did you interview everyone to see if they had left others behind?"

Aidan blustered and stepped backwards, his fear at Cash's ire plain to see.

"I couldn't, your Grace," he mumbled. "We were very busy just trying to make ends meet. Meetings and lists to make and..." his mumbling excuses drew to a stuttering halt.

"You lazy fucking piece of shit," said Cash, his voice low, but throbbing with anger. "There are most likely more survivors out there. I cannot believe you would show no interest whatsoever in that. To not even question the people that came to you for succor."

"We took them in, your Grace. What else was I meant to do?"

"Don't bother looking for an assistant, shithead," commanded Cash. "You are no longer the leader of Redwood. "Now get the hell out of my sight before I kill you."

Aidan hesitated, then turned tail and waddled off.

Cash turned to Sarah. "We need to reorganize this town. You're good with people, take Jed and find out who we could put in charge of this place."

"Hey, you're the one with a 16-point Charisma," said Sarah with a smile. "Maybe you should take a go at talking to them."

Cash stared at Sarah, and just for a moment, she felt the power behind his gaze. The power of a level 32 Duke and Cyberknight.

She bowed hurriedly. "I apologize, your Grace," she said softly. "I was trying to make light of the situation. It won't happen again." She turned to Jed. "Get two of the men and follow me, I need to talk to everyone here."

Cash stood still for a while, his expression a thousand-yard stare. Finally, Bonny nudged his hand and he got the distinct feeling a calm wash over him as she looked at him, her big brown eyes full of compassion.

He scratched her ears. "Sorry, girl," he said quietly. "I just get so mad when I hear of possible survivors that might have died because some useless fuckwit is too lazy or inefficient to help them. Don't they realize that humanity is all we have left. Every life is a gift. It's more important than levels, and credits and fucking System points."

Bonny nodded, and Cash got the image of the people he worked with. Sarah, Jeb, Gunny, Greta and many more.

"Yeah, girl," said Cash. "You get it." He sighed. "Okay, you know what, while Sarah is doing a buttload of in-depth reconnaissance with the local pops, I reckon I'll upgrade this place. Make it a little less of a shithole."

"Arf!"

"Let's start with upgrading the accommodation for the residents. We'll also need a Crafting Hall and a small Barracks to ensure the town's defenses are in order."

Cash's mind focused on the HUD in front of him, as he accessed his System Points. With careful consideration, he allocated the necessary points to initiate the upgrades. The buildings began to transform before their eyes, gaining sturdiness and newfound functionality.

As the town began to undergo its transformation, Cash's attention was drawn to a new option that appeared on his HUD. The opportunity to upgrade the town walls to the next level caught his eye. Knowing the importance of fortifications in this dangerous world, he decided it was a worthy investment.

With a wave of his hand, the town walls rose higher and thicker, gaining an imposing presence. The defenses now matched the upgraded buildings, ensuring the safety and security of Redwood. Then he added four scorpion crossbows and a pair of onagers.

An hour later, Sarah arrived with a half a dozen people in tow.

Cash nodded a greeting. "Okay, so who's my new senior advisor for Redwood?"

Sarah chuckled. "It's a committee," she answered. 'I haven't had time to make a decision. I don't know anyone well enough yet."

Cash shook his head as he stared closely at each of the newcomers.

One of the women curtsied. "Your Grace."

"What's your name?" asked Cash.

"Betty, your Grace."

"Betty, who do you think should lead?"

The woman didn't hesitate. She pointed at a tall, rangy man with a short beard, bald, deep brown eyes and lips that verged on a grin. Much like a porpoise. "Norman, your Grace."

"What about you?"

Betty shook her head. "I'm real good at admin, but I'd make a crappy leader."

"Norman," said Cash. "You wanna be in charge?"

The man shook his head. "Not really, your Grace."

"Tough," responded Cash. "You're the new senior advisor for Redwood. Betty is your 2IC. Between the rest of you, form a council. Got it?"

Norman bowed. "I got it, your Grace."

"I suppose you noticed the upgrades I put in place," continued Cash.

They all nodded. "Good, so we're gonna need someone in charge of the Crafting Hall. Someone else in charge of the military – guards. We call them Peacekeepers in Tomahawk. I haven't built an Adventurers Guild, for now they can share the barracks. And Norman."

"Your Grace."

"When I upgraded the accommodation, I put up a senior advisor's house, as well as a few more slightly more upmarket dwellings for the rest of the council. Sarah, Jeb, you care to show these good people around their new facilities and I'll see you later. I'm gonna walk the walls for a bit."

Sarah bowed and the group left to do Cash's bidding.

"Come on, Bonny, let's check the walls out."

"Arf!"

CHAPTER 25

"You don't think we should have stayed on a bit longer?" asked Sarah.

Cash shook his head. "Norman looks pretty competent. And I think that Betty is as hard as nails. Obviously, they're gonna have a few teething problems, but I'm confident they'll be okay. Which brings me to another thing, when we get back to Tomahawk, I wanna start some sort of diplomatic branch. I'm not talking big, a single person, plus an honor guard. Maybe a carriage and a few horses. Someone who can travel between the towns and keep me updated on how they're all doing. So, get to thinking on it, see if you can come up with someone we could use."

"Will do. What now, we heading home?"

"No, I figured we struck out east, headed towards Coal City. I remember that area well, from when I was a teenager. There used to be a couple of thousand people there. It's time to start checking out bigger places. We need to work our way up to consolidating a few bigger towns. Find larger groups of survivors. My thoughts were to hit Coal City, then a few other towns around there, and after that – Beckley. If memory serves, that was a town with close on twenty thousand souls. Surely there should be a lot of survivors."

"Not necessarily, sir," interjected Higgins. "Large population centers attract large mobs. There is every chance that the city of Beckley has been completely wiped out."

Cash sighed. "Way to have a positive attitude, Higgins. Look at it this way, there's also every chance that they haven't been wiped out. Let's at least hope for the best."

"It's gonna take a few days," added Jeb. "After all, the roads, well what's left of them, are pretty fucked up."

Cash nodded. "Hey, Jeb, who are the fastest two riders we got"

"You and me," answered Jeb.

"Apart from us."

"Pete and Susan."

"Send them back to Tomahawk. Tell them to bring the rest of the cavalry, plus a detachment of twenty Peacekeepers. Meet us at Coal City. We'll take the ride slowly so they'll catch us up."

"Sure thing, your Grace," Jeb hesitated. "You don't think that maybe we'd be taking too many Peacekeepers, be leaving Tomahawk a little low on defense?"

Cash shook his head. "The scorpions and onagers are serious force multipliers. Plus, the Adventures can pitch in if necessary. No worries."

Jeb nodded and wheeled away to inform Pete

and Susan of their mission.

***

Cash and his cavalry detachment took three days to get to the outskirts of Coal City. And the first impression of the town did not fill him with confidence. There were no walls to speak of, and much of the town had been flattened. Small fires burned in various places, thin tendrils of smoke marking each spot.

"Looks like there's no survivors," drawled Jeb.

Cash shook his head. "There are still fires burning. That makes me think that someone is still putting up some sort of resistance. Well, at least it makes me hope they are. Come on, let's take a closer look. Bonny, scout ahead."

The massive Tamaskan took off at a sprint, nose to the ground and ears pricked up.

The rest of the detachment rode into the town two abreast, Jeb and Cash leading, the rest rode behind them. All eyes were peeled, weapons ready.

The streets of Coal City were eerily quiet as they made their way deeper into the town. The only sounds that broke the silence were the hooves of their horses clattering against the cobblestones. The devastation was evident at every turn, and Cash couldn't help but feel a pang of sadness for the lives that were lost here.

Bonny returned to them, her tail wagging slightly. Cash patted her head, understanding the message she conveyed - there were signs of life, but she couldn't find any actual survivors. The tension among the cavalry detachment grew as they continued their search, knowing that they might be the last hope for any remaining townspeople.

They came across a couple of dead steel-wolves and some sort of weird land-octopus, but no human bodies. So they kept searching, dismounting every now and then to check a house or shop.

But no luck.

"The place has been stripped of all foodstuffs," noted Cash. "Tinned foods, sodas, bedding. To me that means someone has survived. We keep looking."

After what felt like an eternity, they came across the entrance to the old coal mines, now fortified with heavy steel doors.

Jeb ran his hand over the doors. "New welding," he said. "These were put up fairly recently. Maybe a few weeks ago."

Cash's eyes narrowed with determination. "I think we may have found where our survivors are hiding out," he said, a glimmer of hope in his voice.

Jeb nodded, a mix of relief and anxiety in his expression. "Let's proceed with caution. It could be a trap, after all."

The detachment dismounted and approached the entrance on foot, their steps measured and wary. Cash placed his hand on the steel door, feeling the cold metal under his touch. "Well, it's not going to open itself," he quipped, but there was an underlying tension in his voice.

"You just can't go smashing them down," said Sarah. "There might be guards with crossbows, children, anything."

"Thanks for stating the obvious," snarked Cash. "I'm not going to blast the fucking things off their hinges, I'll just knock." Using his level 33 Strength he hammered on the door. "Ding dong, Avon calling."

Sarah rolled her eyes. "Sometimes you are such a child," she scoffed. "Also, you bent the doors."

"Don't know my own strength," acknowledged Cash. "Hey, open up," he continued. "Duke Appalachia here, we come to help. Can anyone hear me?"

The detachment waited for a few minutes. Then Cash yelled out again.

"If no one answers, I'll huff and I'll puff and I'll blow these doors down. Come on, guys, I'm a friend. We got food, water, and a real nice town not too far away where you can live in peace ... well, relative peace to be honest. Now, I'm not a patient man, so I'm gonna give you ten seconds, then I'm gonna break the doors down. So, stand back."

There was a slight pause and a male voice called back. "Hah, you try and break those doors down. That's eight inches of hardened steel, with reinforced hinges and…"

The man didn't finish his challenge as Cash finally lost his patience, wound up and punched the door using most of his high-level Strength.

The doors folded in and with a sound of tortured steel overlaid with a massive boom, they rocketed back into the mine.

"Knock knock," said Cash in his best Arnold Schwarzenegger voice.

The opening revealed a group of men and women standing to the side of the door, all had crossbows trained on Cash. A pair of feet stuck out from underneath one of the doors and two more people were laid out flat on the floor, both bleeding and unconscious.

Using his Teleport spell, Cash appeared in front of the group of six crossbow wielding survivors and, in under a second, he had disarmed them.

The rest of the detachment moved forward and physically apprehended them while Cash continued onwards to cast Healing on the pair of prone bodies.

He then flicked the door aside to reveal a badly damaged man. His arms were obviously fractured, his ribs appeared to be broken as well, and blood poured from a deep laceration on his forehead. Cash cast Healing on him as fast as he could until the bones popped back into place and the open wounds sealed up.

Finally, Cash stood and faced the survivors.

"Right, sorry about the dramatic entrance, but you fuckers just wouldn't listen. Now, no harm done, I've healed up any injuries. This dude here will take a little while to recover, but give him an hour or so and he'll be back to being a moron in no time. Who is in charge?"

One of the women pointed at the unconscious man. "Mickey."

"Yeah, apart from him," said Cash. "Mickey appears to be a little under the weather right now."

"Then I suppose it would be me," acknowledged the woman. "I'm Dolly."

"Cool, I am Cash Stone, you may have seen a few System announcements about me."

"He is the Duke of Appalachia," interjected Sarah. "So, a big cheese in these parts."

"In all parts, actually, lady Sarah," added Higgins.

Dolly looked a little overwhelmed. "I...oh... hello, sir."

'Your Grace," said Sarah. "That's how you address a fancy-pants duke."

"Sorry, your Grace," Dolly corrected. "How may we be of service?"

"Talk to me," commanded Cash. "We want to help. Give me the run down – how many of you are there? Do you have food and water? Can we heal anyone else? What are your plans? And finally, what the fuck happened here. Actually, start with that last question, then show us around."

***

Turned out that the experience of the residents of Coal City was little different to any other survivors Cash had come across. The countdown ended and then the shit hit the fan. Waves of monsters, wholesale death and destruction. But the townsfolk had managed to band together rather quickly and board themselves up in the old abandoned mines. Apparently, that was largely due to the leadership of the town mayor, a mister Jacob Dean. The problem was, Jacob died a couple of weeks before, and there was no one as competent to take his place.

Jacob had organized foraging and hunting parties, gotten people to collect water, and generally kept as good a state of order as he could. Then he had been killed by a troop of some type of hybrid monkey-beetle things while out on a hunt.

Mickey had put himself forward as the next leader, and things had gone downhill from there. Not that Cash blamed the man, after all, no one else had stepped up to the plate. It wasn't his fault that he was incompetent. Although maybe if he had wanted to lead, he should have actually done so.

As Dolly led them all further into the mine, Cash found his heart pounding with every step. The darkness seemed to swallow them whole as they ventured deeper into the mines. The walls were rough and uneven, and the smell of coal and dampness filled their nostrils.

As they progressed, they noticed signs of recent activity - discarded food containers, makeshift bedding, and faint footprints on the dusty ground. The feeling of defeat and sadness hung in the air like a miasma. If loss had an aroma, it was the smell permeating this dank underground refuge.

After what felt like an eternity, they reached a large underground chamber. And there were the survivors of Coal City. Men, women, and children, their faces lined with weariness and fear, looked up at Cash and his detachment with a mixture of relief and apprehension. There must have been over a hundred of them.

Before Dolly could introduce him, Cash stepped forward and poke, his voice low and reassuring. All 16 of his Charisma points hammering home.

"I am Cash Stone, the Duke of Appalachia," he said, his voice throbbing with power and reassurance. "My detachment and I are here to offer our assistance. It's not safe for you to remain here. You will come with us to my capital city of Tomahawk. There I will provide food, water, power, accommodation and safety. Welcome to you all."

One of the men, an older man with pale blue eyes and a serious stoop nodded, his eyes filled with gratitude. "We've been hiding down here for ages, ever since the monsters attacked. We thought we were the last ones left."

"No, sir," stated Cash. "There are many of us, and there is one thing I can guarantee, from this moment on your lives will be infinitely better. Now tell me," Cash continued as he turned to Dolly. "Who needs healing?"

CHAPTER 26

Cash spent two days ensuring that all of the survivors were healed up, fed and clothed. By the end of the two days, they were all probably in better condition than they had been since the beginning of the apocalypse.

By then his second cavalry detachment had arrived along with twenty-three peacekeepers. Cash sent the survivors back to Tomahawk with two of the cavalry and eight Peacekeepers to protect them. Much to Sarah's chagrin, he told her to accompany them as well. She had argued but he had convinced her that the one hundred plus survivors needed a strong leader, plus someone capable of adding high-power ranged attacks to keep them safe.

She couldn't think of an argument that trumped his, so, reluctantly, she had agreed.

After they had seen the survivors safely off, Cash got Jeb, Caleb and lieutenant Jack Pension together to discuss their next move.

"I wanna go to Crab Orchard and then Beckley," stated Cash.

"Beckley is a pretty big town," noted Jack.

"We've been taking on places with sub three thousand populations, and Beckley is closer to twenty thousand."

"Yep, and if we had enough people I'd go for a place like Charleston. But that's a bit ambitious, so we'll have to wait and consolidate a bit."

"Whatever you say, your Grace," confirmed Jack.

"We head out tomorrow morning at first light. It'll take a few days to get to Crab Orchard, we'll reassess the situation after we see exactly what's happening there."

Everyone nodded their agreement and then headed for a bit of shut-eye, except of course those on sentry duty.

***

The column made its way through the thick forest. Cash marveled at the fact that the trees had gotten even larger. The System had instituted a growth routine that now meant that some trees were as high as small skyscrapers and as large around as well. Truly magnificent.

As they moved, Bonny ran up next to Cash and nudged his leg. Cash immediately got a rush of separate impressions from his canine companion. The order was a little jumbled, but the message was clear.

Cash halted and waited for Jack to catch up.

"We're being watched,' He informed his lieutenant quietly. "Bonny reckons at least five or six men, up ahead, some at ground level, a couple up in the trees."

"The dog told you that?" questioned Jack.

"Bonny is more than just a dog," said Cash. "And yes, trust me, Bonny's scouting abilities are second to none."

"You reckon it's an ambush?" asked Jack.

"Bonny gave me the impression that they were carrying bows and spears. Lightly armored. Almost like a forward scouting unit. I would be surprised if they actually sprung any sort of ambush. They're outnumbered and outgunned, so to speak."

"What are your suggestions, your Grace."

Cash shrugged. "I'll just ride forward and confront them," he answered.

"Too risky," disagreed Jack. "You're the duke. Maybe Jeb, or Caleb or I should do that."

Cash chuckled. "No risk. Even if they fire arrows at me, there's very little chance any will get past a few bolts of lightning. And if a half dozen men attack me, well let's just say, they'll find themselves totally outnumbered by a force of one."

That said, Cash spurred Stanley and rode forward, Bonny by his side.

"Bonny, tell me when we get close," he said.

"Arf!"

As they rode closer to the spot Bonny had indicated, Cash's senses were on high alert. He could feel the tension in the air, the anticipation of a possible confrontation. The forest seemed to hold its breath, waiting to see what would unfold.

Sure enough, as they reached a small clearing, four men emerged from the shadows, their expressions wary and defensive. They held bows and spears, their eyes fixed on Cash as he approached.

Cash noticed that although they were wearing a mixture of post-apocalyptic armor and pre-RPG military issue body armor, they all sported Marine Corps badges and insignia. A quick scan of the group allowed him to pick out the senior Marine.

"Corporal," he greeted the man. "Tell your men in the trees to stand down before they make me nervous and I have to explain the facts of life to them."

"You don't give me or my men orders."

Cash shook his head, then he fired off a lightning bolt, striking a nearby tree and blowing a huge smoldering hole in it. "Don't kick things off by being a dickhead. Tell them to stand down, or I will make them stand down. And just fucking relax, we mean no harm. We're simply on a fact-finding mission. On our way to Crab Orchard to see if there are any survivors and offer them some help."

"Why the fuck should we believe you?" asked the corporal, his voice full of aggression.

Cash met the man's gaze with a calm demeanor, dismounting from Stanley and holding up a hand in a gesture of peace. "My name is Cash Stone, Duke of Appalachia. And you should believe me because I have no reason to lie to you. And if we meant any harm, we could have already wiped the floor with you," he said, his voice carrying a firm authority.

The Marine's eyes widened with surprise at Cash's title, but he didn't lower his weapon. "How do you know there aren't more of us?"

Cash laughed. "There aren't."

The Marine studied Cash and the rest of his group for a few seconds, then he called out. "Knowles, Jamison, get down here."

There was a scuffle in the trees and two men clambered down, their bows slung over their shoulders.

"So, how do I address a Duke?"

"Officially, your Grace," answered Cash. "But sir will do as well."

"You an officer?"

Cash sneered. "Rangers. Sergeant. I worked for a living, son, so don't insult me. Jack over there is a lieutenant, army. So, if you feel the need to salute anyone, he's your man."

"Sorry for the reception," said the corporal. "We've learned not to trust strangers in these lands. I'm corporal Jarvis."

Cash nodded, understanding the caution. "Fair enough. Let me introduce myself and my companions." He gestured to the cavalry and the Peacekeepers. "We are survivors, just like you. Our town of Tomahawk has been growing and thriving, as have my towns of Redwood and

Peach hamlet. And we're looking to establish connections with other surviving communities."

The Marine eyed them warily. "How do we know you're not just another group of raiders?"

"Oh for fuck sakes," grunted Cash. "Stop being such a fucking crayon-eater. We're here to help. If we were raiders, we would have capped your asses already. Now do you want to join us, maybe come with us to Crab Orchard?"

"Two things, your Grace," drawled Jarvis. "I don't appreciate being called a crayon-eater by some dope-on-a-rope, even if he is a duke. And secondly, it'll do you no good going to Crab Orchard, because it don't exist no more."

"What?"

"You heard me, sir. We're all originally from Crab Orchard." The Marine's expression darkened. "After the apocalypse, the town sort of survived, actually did pretty well. We built a wall out of scrap, consolidated. Managed to get a well dug, hunt for food. It wasn't great, but we were surviving. Then a few weeks later, we were attacked by a large force of humans. The battle lasted for days, and in the end, our town was destroyed. We managed to escape, but the rest of the townsfolk were either killed, or taken prisoner and led away to Beckley."

Cash's heart sank at the news. "Beckley, you say? So the city is controlled by bandits?"

The Marine shook his head. "It's more complicated than that. From the reconnaissance we've done, the city seems to have split into a number of different factions. We're not sure who's in charge of what faction, but there's a lot of fighting. It's a dangerous place to be. And we don't have enough men to do anything about it all."

Cash though for a few seconds then nodded. "I need to take a closer look at Beckley. You boys in or out?"

"We're in," confirmed Jarvis. "To be honest, we're all a bit sick of hanging around doing nothing. It's time to fuck shit up."

Cash laughed. "Well, you know what they say, if you absolutely have to have some shit fucked up in quick time, call the Marines."

"Oorah, duke," shouted Jarvis.

"Oorah," echoed his men.

CHAPTER 27

"There's no walls," said Cash.

Jarvis raised an eyebrow. "What the fuck do you call those things?" he asked, pointing at the eight feet high pile of rubble and furniture that surrounded the enclave.

"I call that a pile of shit," answered Cash. "That ain't no wall. That's just trash piled into a heap."

"Well, what did you expect?" asked Jarvis. "Machinery don't work no more. No trucks to carry stuff, no cranes. That's actually a pretty good wall. You telling me you got better ones around your towns?"

"Your Grace," snapped lieutenant Jack.

"What?"

"You will refer to the duke as, your Grace," stated Jack. "The world may have gone to shit, but in this man's army we still adhere to discipline and respect, Marine."

Jarvis looked abashed. "Sorry, sir. Your Grace."

"And for your information, corporal," continued Jack. "The walls around Tomahawk are made of cut stone, over twenty feet high and twelve feet thick. They have mana powered gates, watchtowers with scorpion crossbows and onager catapults, and the entire structure is surrounded by a deep moat with a drawbridge. The smaller towns of Peach Haven and Redwood are similar."

Jarvis did a double take. "No shit?"

"No shit, Marine," confirmed Jack.

"How the hell did you manage that?"

"It's not important right now," interjected Cash. "What is important is that none of these fuckers are a high enough level to earn and use System points. All they have in their favor is numbers. But even that is negated by the fact that they've split up and are warring against each other like a bunch of medieval landlords. Fucking idiots, can't they see that human life is the most important thing right now. Not power, or ownership. People."

"What do we do now, your Grace?" asked Jack.

"More recon," answered Cash. "I want to get closer to each of the enclaves. We know that there are five of them. Do we know who attacked Crab Orchard? Which enclave is the strongest? Who has the most combat ready bodies? Food, water, all that crap. Once we know more, then we can plan."

***

"I think we should designate the enclaves alphabetically," said Jack. "Alpha, Beta, Charlie, Delta and Echo."

"What's wrong with my tags?" asked Cash with a smirk. "They're also alphabetic."

"Nothing, your Grace. It's just that Asshole, Buttocks, Cockface, Dildo and Elfdick don't sound very professional."

"Yeah, I'm not even sure Elfdick is a word," added Jeb.

"Fine," conceded Cash. "Take all the fun out of it." He looked at the crudely drawn map. "Designate them clockwise. Now, what have we found out?" he asked Jarvis who had sent his men on an extensive recon mission.

Beta are definitely the asswipes who attacked us and took our people prisoner," said Jarvis. "My boys managed to spot at least two of the survivors."

"Good," said Cash. "So, we know that they are at the top of our shit list. What else?"

Jarvis continued to relay all of the info the Marines had collected, ranging from population to weapons, weaknesses in the walls and the various sentry movements.

"Can we make contact with any of them?' mused Cash.

Jack shrugged. "Maybe, but the likelihood is that all of the factions are unfriendly. If they weren't then it seems reasonable to deduce that they would have banded together. Looks to me that they're in a standoff situation. From the reports, they all look to be of similar sizes and strengths. I think it would be simpler if we just hit Beta, took them out of the equation and claim the area as our own."

"I concur," agreed Cash. He turned to Jarvis. "Any ideas?"

"Yeah, we wait until nightfall, then we sneak in and fuck shit up."

Cash chuckled. "Simple and to the point, but I think we can extrapolate on that a little. Here's what I reckon."

And Cash told them his plan to take enclave Beta.

CHAPTER 28

The wall around enclave Beta consisted mainly of scrapped motor vehicles, supplemented with blocks of masonry and random pieces of furniture. The gate itself was a school bus. And to open it, the guards simply rolled it out the way, then pushed it back to close the gap.

Cash had stationed the cavalry behind a row of derelict houses about two hundred yards in front of the gate. Then he got Jack to move the Peacekeepers closer, splitting them into two equal groups and taking cover in the piles of detritus around the gate. One on each side, about forty yards out.

Then Cash entrusted Jarvis and his Marines to infiltrate the enclave through a small gap in the makeshift wall, some hundred yards south of the gate.

The aim was for them to make their way to the gate, dispatch the gate guards and push the bus to the side. Then the cavalry and the Peacekeepers would charge in and, as Jarvis said, fuck shit up.

To help them achieve their goal, Cash and Bonny had taken up position on the opposite side of the enclave. From here, Cash would cause a distraction. A bombardment of mana bolts and lightning strikes to garner the enclaves undivided attention. Then after the gates were opened, he would teleport into the enclave and help his people to create the necessary mayhem. He trusted that Bonny would follow, as she would easily be able to either scale the wall or simply muscle her way through.

Cash scratched Bonny between her ears and readied himself for the onslaught.

***

Derek ran his tongue over his chapped lips. He couldn't remember the last time he had enough water to drink his fill. The constant thirst and ever-present hunger were like a cancer, whittling away his will to live.

Life had truly gone to shit since those fucking Overlords had turned the world into their own goddam computer game.

And after the monsters had been driven off, the people turned on each other. Survivors killing survivors. It made no sense to Derek. Surely now was the time to help each other out. To get together and stand as a united front.

But instead, man's inhumanity to man came to the forefront.

Jesus, only a few days ago, Chief Manning, had taken half of the soldiers and raided the town of Crab Orchard. Why? Fuck knows. But they had been victorious, killing most of them and bringing back a fair number of female slaves.

It made Derek wanna hurl. But he just kept his head down and said nothing.

Because Chief Manning did not take kindly to criticism, either imagined or inferred.

People who spoke out against the Chief, and even many that didn't, found themselves in a shallow grave, with their heads decorating a pike next to the gates of the settlement.

But there was nothing Derek could do to stop the process. He was nineteen years old, his entire family had died in the first few days, and all he could do was team up with any group that would have him.

Now here he was, patrolling the walls.

Thirsty, hungry and disgusted with humanity as a whole.

But particularly with that psychopath in charge, Chief Manning.

Derek stopped at the end of his designated area, nodding a greeting to the sentry in the next quadrant. And as he turned to retrace his steps...

...all hell broke loose.

A series of bright blue mana bolts thumped against the wall, exploding with great force, throwing one of the cars high into the air as it did. Then a salvo of lighting thundered down, raking across the wall and surrounds like a second world war artillery barrage.

"Holy shit," yelled Derek as he hit the ground

hard, curling up into a fetal position as burning bits of wood and furniture rained down around him. He waited for the onslaught to die down, but it didn't. The ground shook as thunderbolt after thunderbolt hammered into the wall. The sound of running footsteps and men shouting orders intruded on his hearing and he finally looked up to see loads of sentries converging on him, their spears and swords at the ready.

Derek peered across at his neighboring sentry, but when he saw him, there was little left but a smoldering pile of burned flesh. He had obviously taken a direct hit from one of the lightning bolts. Derek tried to remember the dudes name, but he couldn't.

Finally, he decided to stand up. Not that he could do anything against this unholy baptism of fire, but simply because if he got to his feet, he would find it easier to run away.

And that is exactly what he did. Fuck Chief Manning, fuck the whole lot of them with their warmongering, and prison taking and generally asshole-ness. Derek had enough. So, he ran, looking for a place to lie low until this, whatever the fuck this was, was over.

CHAPTER 29

Cash threw another series of lightning bolts at the makeshift wall, then he unleashed a barrage of mana bolts from his crossbow. He could hear the sound of men shouting, screaming in pain, footsteps slamming against the ground as they ran.

"Well, Bonny, I figure we've attracted enough attention, I wonder how the boys are doing?"

The Marines had infiltrated the enclave with ease, and they were currently using Cash's distraction to full effect. After dropping two guards, they had pushed the bus to the side and opened up the entrance. As soon as the bus was out the way, the cavalry and the Peacekeepers charged, flooding into the enclave like a tide of vengeance.

At the same time, Cash teleported inside, and Bonny followed by simply jumping over what was left of the wall.

It was absolute mayhem.

The Peacekeepers formed a wall, shields locked and spears forward as they marched across the enclave. The cavalry split into two equal forces and flanked the Peacekeepers, attacking anyone who dared try to stop them.

Although Cash's forces were outnumbered at least five to one, the numbers made little difference. A rag-tag bunch of bandits, half starved, dehydrated and untrained, against a well-equipped, well trained, highly motivated professional outfit.

The fight, if it could even be called that, came to an abrupt end soon after Cash came across Chief Manning.

The Chief himself was quite a sight to behold. Almost seven feet tall, build like a brick shithouse, plate armor and a massive spear with a double-wide blade, he appeared to be a fearsome warrior.

He was flanked by four personal bodyguards, also men of a higher caliber than anyone else in the enclave.

Cash did a quick Identify and noted the man was Level 22. Higgins flickered into shape next to Cash for a few seconds. "Sir, I note that that man has invested almost all of his points into Strength. So, I would recommend that you avoid being struck by him. It would literally be like being run over by a freight train."

"Thanks, Higgins. Good advice, but you forgot to tell me to concentrate on his weak spots."

"Really, sir. You feel that this is a good time to josh with me?"

Cash chuckled. "Just pulling your chain, Higgins. Thanks for the assistance. Bonny, kill those bodyguards."

"Arf!"

"Hey, troll boy," yelled Cash. "Shouldn't you be living under a bridge somewhere, instead of bothering us humans?"

The Chief stared at Cash and then let out a loud battle cry. "Time to die, little man," he shouted as he shook his spear at Cash.

Bonny sprinted forward, leaping between the bodyguards, ripping and tearing at them with great speed and ferocity. Biting, then moving, a blur of speed they were unable to keep up with.

"You dare invade my city," yelled the Chief.

"City?" scoffed Cash. "I would hardly call this collection of hovels a city. Now look, I'm gonna give you one chance, surrender, become my vassal, and we'll all live happily ever after. Or don't, and you won't live out the night. Actually, your expiry date will come up in the next few minutes."

The Chief bellowed incoherently and charged.

Cash hit him with a lightning bolt, then peppered him with four quick mana bolts. The Chief staggered, his charge turning into a lurching wobble as he was hammered by enough power to down an elephant. But his strength was so high, that he managed to shrug the attack off and keep coming forward.

Cash also moved forward, equipping his ax as he did.

The Chief lunged, attempting to skewer Cash with the massive blade of his spear. But to Cash, the movement was so slow and clumsy as to be almost comical.

"Shit," grunted Cash to himself. "I thought this might turn out to be a worthwhile fight. But this lumbering fool is pathetic."

"I heard that," screamed the Chief. "Pathetic? Well take this." He swung his blade at Cash, the spear whistling through the air as it descended.

Cash stepped to the side, and with a casual swing, lopped the Chiefs right arm off at the elbow.

The giant warrior stared at his dismembered limb for a full second before he squealed in agony. "You chopped off my arm," he screeched.

"Are you sure?" asked Cash. "Oh, yes, looks like I did. I'd say sorry, but that would be a lie. Now, do you submit?"

"You chopped off my fucking arm," repeated the Chief in an accusatory tone. "You fucking asshole."

"Hey," retorted Cash. "You were trying to kill me."

"Fuck you."

Cash shook his head. "Okay, fine. Whatever." The ax swung again. This time the Chief's head leaped from his shoulders as the butterfly shaped blade beheaded him with a single blow. Blood jetted high as the body fell sideways and hit the floor.

Cash turned to check how Bonny was doing. But she was fine. Sitting on her haunches, while all around her lay the still bodies of the ex-Chief's now dead bodyguards.

And as Cash surveyed the battle, he could see that it was as good as over. The Beta enclave residents were throwing down their weapons and raising their hands in surrender. There was still the odd pocket of resistance, but mere minutes later, the Peacekeepers and the cavalry were shepherding everyone to the middle of the enclave.

The battle was over. Now it was time to talk.

***

Turned out the residents of Beta enclave were all more than happy to swear an oath to Cash. Apparently, the Chief wasn't well liked at all. But in times of great strife, people often turn to whoever is the strongest to lead. Even if those are also the biggest assholes amongst them.

But even though the Chief had ruled with an iron fist, he was pretty useless at management, providing food, water, or actually anything. His vision was more Viking Raider, than town planner.

Now all anyone wanted was just to be safe, have enough water, some food, a roof over their heads. And not to have those same heads on a pike at the gate.

Simple wants, but in a world gone mad, ones needs become fewer.

After the requisite oaths had been taken, Cash received a raft of System messages. He read through them and then called for Higgins, who once again simply materialized out of thin air next to him.

"Higgins, the System won't let me upgrade this place."

Higgins frowned. "I'm sure you should be able to, sir."

"No," denied Cash. "I tried to select city walls, and the option is grayed out. Likewise with water, mana power. Actually everything. That sucks."

"I think you need to drill down further into the menu, sir," advised Higgins. "After all, this enclave is not a city, it is merely a part of the old city. A suburb perhaps. I think if you look for the options available to create either an outpost, or perhaps a stronghold you might find some options available."

Cash did as Higgins said, and a minute later he grinned. "Cool, found it."

"What's the plan, your Grace?" asked lieutenant Jack.

"I'm gonna put some proper walls around this enclave," answered Cash. "Then I'll get some water, mana power, a few scorpions and onagers. Then once we're obviously the seat of power around her, we can start some negotiations with the rest of the idiots in the other enclaves, maybe consolidate this back into a town."

"Sir," interjected Higgins. "If I may, I urge you to show some serious urgency to the upgrades."

"Why?"

"I sense a beast wave coming. At least a few hundred mobs. Once again, I feel the System is reacting in an unusually aggressive manner. Almost as if it is testing you personally."

"Done, thanks, Higgins." Cash concentrated on his HUD and minutes later the landscape around them shimmered and the ground shook as the System instituted Cash's changes.

"Jack, get the Peacekeepers together. Also, muster anyone who has a ranged weapon, bow, crossbow, a fucking slingshot. I want them all on the walls. Get your people to man the onagers and the scorpions. Jeb, Caleb, Your guys on the walls as well. But keep the horses ready. We may need to ride out at some stage. I'm gonna go to the top of the watchtower next to the gate and unleash a few thunderbolts on the mobs. You'll got that?'

"Yes, your Grace," chorused the officers.

"Bonny, stay down, keep an eye out for any mob that makes it over the walls. You see one, take it out."

"Arf!"

Cash made his way to the watchtower, moving at pace. As soon as he got to the top, he could already see the first wave of beasts approaching. He immediately fired a few mana bolts from his crossbow at them. Even though they were right at the edge of his range. Because he wasn't actually looking to do any damage, he was more trying to attract attention to the incoming horded in the hope that the other enclaves would see it and get a bit of warning.

He could see the Peacekeeper crews readying

the onagers and the giant scorpion crossbows. He wondered how much ammunition they had. He had equipped loads of the machines to his various towns, and although he knew they came with a stock of ammo, he had no idea how much.

"Higgins."

His AI manifested next to him.

"How much ammunition does the System supply when it equips the siege weapons?"

"I'm not sure on the exact quantities, sir. But suffice to say, none of them have ever run out in any prior battles."

"Okay, good to know," noted Cash. "So, that's one less thing to worry about." He rolled his neck and stretched. "Here they come," he said quietly to.

The ground beneath Cash's feet rumbled as the approaching wave of beasts drew nearer. From his vantage point in the watchtower, he could see the horde stretching out as far as the eye could see. Mutant creatures of all shapes and sizes, driven by an insatiable hunger for destruction, charged toward the walls of the newly upgraded stronghold.

The defenders on the walls readied their weapons, their faces determined, and the air was charged with anticipation. Hundreds of arrows, bolts, and spears were aimed at the approaching mass of beasts. The onagers and scorpions were loaded, their crews standing ready to unleash a barrage of deadly projectiles.

With a deep breath, Cash raised his hand,

crackling with lightning. His mana crossbow hummed with power, and he unleashed a series of thunderbolts at the lead creatures of the approaching horde. The lightning tore through the beasts, electrifying the air and leaving a trail of smoldering bodies.

As the first wave of the attack drew closer, the defenders on the walls released a volley of arrows and bolts, cutting down dozens of the creatures. But the horde was relentless, and soon the walls were swarmed with snarling beasts, clambering over each other in their desperate attempt to breach the defenses.

The onagers and scorpions fired, their projectiles raining down on the mass of beasts, causing chaos and destruction among the mutant mob's ranks. Yet, still, the horde pressed on.

Cash's heart pounded in his chest as he continued to unleash lightning bolts on the beasts, his mana reserves depleting with each attack. He knew he had to be strategic in his use of power, as he couldn't afford to exhaust himself too quickly.

"Steady, everyone! Hold the line!" Jack's commanding voice echoed across the walls, rallying the defenders to stand firm against the onslaught.

A few extremely agile monkey-mutants managed to scale the wall and leap into the compound. But as soon as they touched the ground, Bonny was on them, ripping and tearing.

As the first wave of beasts began to thin out,

Cash saw movement in the distance. Smoke rising from the other enclaves indicated that they too were under attack. Without hesitation, he made a decision.

"Jeb, Caleb, with me! We ride out to the other enclaves. The cavalry will break through the beasts ranks! It's time to take the fight to them."

The cavalry detachment readied themselves, their eyes burning with determination. With a powerful surge, they burst through the gates and charged into the mass of beasts. Spears and lances skewered the creatures, while crossbows and bows shot them down from a distance.

Cash's ax gleamed in the sunlight as he swung it with deadly precision, clearing a path for the others to follow. He could feel the adrenaline coursing through his veins as he unleashed his power, lightning bolts striking down enemies left and right.

The cavalry carved a path through the horde, reaching the other enclaves just in time, charging in, slaughtering and then wheeling away and on to the next enclave. Providing enough destruction to enable the defenders to turn the tide by themselves.

The survivors within the walls cheered as they saw Cash and his companions arrive, coming to their aid. With the combined forces of the cavalry and the survivors, they fought back against the attacking beasts with renewed vigor.

Back at Cash's stronghold, the defenders were

holding their ground, the onagers and scorpions continuing to wreak havoc on the remaining waves of enemies. The tide of battle began to turn in their favor as the beasts' numbers dwindled.

And then, it was over.

"Jeb, Caleb. Losses?"

"Two," said Jeb. "Another six injured, but both Caleb and me got Healing, so they'll pull through."

"Who'd we lose?"

"Carter and Pauline."

"Shit," a wave of guilt crashed over Cash. He had ordered the charge. It was his fault they were dead. He took a deep breath. "I'm sorry."

"It's war, your Grace," said Caleb. "People die. We all know that. Ain't nothing to be sorry about. We'll be sad, then we'll remember them, but we'll move on."

"True," said Cash. "Thanks. Now, I need to see whoever is in charge of the other enclaves. I have a feeling that they'll all be a bit more open to talking than they would have been yesterday."

"And then some, your Grace. Them fuckers all owe us now," said Jeb.

"Yep, do me a favor, Jeb. Go get Jack, give him a horse, then the four of us will do the rounds. It's time to get political."

CHAPTER 30

Cash had been correct in his assumption that the general reception and good will towards him and his men would be better than it would have before.

But his usual theory about there always being at least one major asshole also proved correct.

He visited each of the enclaves in turn, Alpha, Charlie, Delta and Echo. First, he spoke to the leaders of each enclave, then he convinced them to all meet at his stronghold.

Three of the leaders and their respective advisors agreed to put forward the concept of vassalage to their people. It actually wasn't a difficult decision. One look at the upgraded stronghold with its hot running water, mana powered, new accommodation and walls made all of the other enclaves look like unsanitary refugee camps.

And as Cash explained, if they all took the oath, he now had enough System points to upgrade the entire town, walling the whole area, putting in a moat, and running a road to his other towns.

Alpha, Charlie and Echo agreed.

The leader of enclave Delta, Tom Cobb, demanded he be made co-leader and be given the rank of earl at least.

Delta was no larger than any of the other enclaves, each of them containing around three hundred people. It had no advantages, no superior resources and no stronger military presence. What it did have was a proper dyed in the wool asshole in charge. A man more interested in his own personal power than in the wellbeing of his people.

Cash tried. He argued, he cajoled and he even begged. He explained that the System gave ranks and System points. It had nothing to do with him.

But Cobb simply folded his arms and shook his head.

Finally, Cobb stood up and poked Cash in the chest. "Listen, mister high and fucking mighty, you do as I say, or this whole deal is off. I will go back to my people and I will tell them that all you want to do is enslave us. We will fight you to the last man, woman and child."

"But if I accede to your demands?" asked Cash.

"Then I will go back and tell them that you are a good man and they must all swear the oath."

Cash thought for a bit. He considered asking Jack, Jeb and Caleb for advice, but he didn't, because he knew that whatever the decision, it was his alone. And any consequences should, and must be his to carry.

"Cobb," said Cash as he stood up. "You are a bad person. You do not care about anything but yourself. And that is fine, except now that selfishness is going to harm others. So, I reject your ultimatum."

"Well, your loss, dickhead," yelled Cobb. "We'll see what my people have to say about that."

"No," said Cash as he equipped his ax. "We won't."

Cash swung, and Cobb's headless corpse fell to the floor.

"I need to talk to the people of enclave Delta," said Cash. "The rest of you, go to your people. Come on, we got a city to upgrade."

***

There were nineteen holdouts spread amongst the residents of what used to be the thriving city of Beckley. Cash spoke to each of them personally in an attempt to get them to take the oath. He explained that he also swore an oath, he told them they wouldn't be slaves. He did his best. But even with his now burgeoning Charisma stat, he only managed to convince three of them to change their minds. The other sixteen were summarily banished.

Then Cash checked his HUD.

"Holy crap, Higgins," he exclaimed. "For some reason I've been awarded an absolute shithouse full of System points."

"Well, sir, you have added a town of over a thousand residents to your portfolio. Plus, you helped defeat a vast beast wave, and expanded the territory you control. All in all, it seems to me that it is right and proper the System throws you a bone or two."

"Dude, it's like 600 points. Also, there's more weapons, additional upgrades, and a System Shop. How come I get another shop? I thought you had to have a dungeon to get a shop."

"No, sir," answered Higgins. "That is one of the requirements. However, sometimes the System decides that a town of over one thousand residents may also get a shop. It is unusual, but not unheard of. As I said before, after the Integration the rules will most likely change."

"Right, let's do some serious shopping," said Cash rubbing his hands together like some sort of avaricious money lender.

Half an hour later, the town of New Beckley was surrounded by a level three wall, some twenty-five feet high and eighteen feet thick, together with twelve watchtowers, a front and rear gate. A full water filled moat with drawbridges, portcullises and sally port defenses. The walls and watchtowers sported the usual scorpion crossbows and onagers, but Cash had also installed a pair of trebuchets in the keep. Two large boulder firing siege weapons with a range almost four times further than the onagers. There were also braziers with metal buckets filled with pitch at various points along the wall, ready to be heated and pour their heated contents on any attackers below.

Cash had also gone full out on the interior of the town. Accommodation, including a number of Senior Advisor dwellings. A Barracks, an Adventurers Guild, a Crafting Hall, a Greenhouse and a separate Blacksmiths building.

He hadn't included any fancy accommodation for himself, as he planned on moving along as soon as things were sorted. And anyway, Cash considered Tomahawk to be his homebase, even if it was smaller than New Beckley.

Finally, he installed a road from Beckley to his other towns.

Cash appointed five Senior Advisors and allowed them to choose two assistants each. Then he oversaw a meeting where they allocated the various sections of the town to whomever they considered the best fit. A man in charge of the Peacekeepers, a woman in charge of the Adventurers guild, others in charge of crafting, farming, blacksmithing and so on.

Finally, Cash visited the new System Shop, together with Higgins. The rest of his people also wanted to sell loot to the shop, but Cash had placed himself at the head of the queue, followed by his Peacekeepers and his cavalry, as they needed to get on their way as soon as possible.

As usual, Cash simply dumped the contents of his Inventory on the long counter, and then let Higgins do the bargaining.

Cash was surprised at how much stuff he had accumulated over the many recent battles.

He was even more surprised when Higgins informed him of the final amount of credits he was due.

"Three hundred and eighty thousand credits. Cool," stated Cash. "I wonder what that would be in dollars?"

"There is no possible exchange rate for that," said Higgins.

"I know," grunted Cash. "But for the sake of argument, and to make me feel good, I'm gonna put the exchange rate from System Credits to Dollars at 110 to one. So that means I got like over forty million Dollars right now."

"Sir, I really think…"

"Higgy-baby."

"Sorry, sir. Well done on becoming a Dollar multimillionaire. What are you going to do with the money?"

"Reckon I'll get these guys a bunch of armor, weapons and shit. Also, maybe see if I can get some sort of hi-tech wagon so we can transport an onager, or a couple of scorpions. We got spare horses, would be nice to have some artillery."

"Excellent idea, sir. May I ask, have you checked out your points and stats yet?"

Cash sighed. "No. I just know those Overlord fuckers will have chucked another Charisma point at me."

"Sir, I seriously have no idea why you are so averse to upping your Charisma. I think it may be because you do not really know what Charisma does, especially when it gets to higher double figures."

"I know," snapped Cash. "Makes you likeable. Life and soul of the party shit. Never really seen the point of that. If you have enough in common with someone, you become friends. Don't need some stat to back that up."

"Yes, it does help in social situations," admitted Higgins. "But it is also essential to good strong leadership. And when you get it higher, it does so much more. Charisma stats exceeding 20 begin to allow you to influence a person's thinking. Over 50 and it verges on mind control. Not that you would use that on friends or allies, but you can literally make a lower-level enemy put down his weapons if you will it so."

"Is that so?"

"Yes," confirmed Higgins. "That is so."

"You're right, I did not appreciate that," admitted Cash as he pulled up his points and stats. "Yep, fuckers upped my Charisma by 2 more points. I'm on 18 now. Gained 3 levels, now on 35, so I got 6 points to allocate. Few more upgrades to weapons, spells and stuff. Oh well, I'm gonna run with Charisma, up it to 20. Then I'll spread the rest about a bit."

Cash allocated his points.

"Hey, Higgins, how come Bonny is so many levels behind me? I thought we rose together."

"Animal companions rise at a much slower rate, sir. But mark my words, she is extremely powerful. You cannot simply take her Strength and Agility as any sort of reliable yardstick. Her intelligence makes her a much more formidable opponent than any simple beast at the same, or even at a much higher level."

"Cool," responded Cash. "Okay, time to buy some stuff for these dudes. Then I need to get together with Jack, Caleb and Jeb, figure what to do next."

He ran an eye over his Character Sheet as he headed off to find his officers.

Name: Cash Stone	Class: Cyberknight Level: 35	Experience Points XP 4500000 (5000000)	Hit Points HP 1000 (50) (40 per minute)	Stamina ST 1000 (40 per minute)		Mana Points MP 700 (30 per minute)
Strength 34	Constitution 33	Agility 32	Dexterity 7	Mind 37		Charisma 20
System Points 320			Credits 500000			
Weapons – Elemental Ax – Level 10 Cybernetic crossbow – Level 9						
Perks – Personal cybernetic enhancements – Level 9 Cybernetic Armor – Level 9						
Titles – Ursine Exterminator Eager Beaver Duke Appalachia Giant Killer						
Spells – Lightning Bolt – Level 10 Healing – 6 Teleport – 4						
Companions – Bonny Stone Boss Hunter Level: 16	Hit Points HP 550 (14 per Minute)	Strength 21		Constitution 20	Agility 20	Mind 8

CHAPTER 31

"Honestly, your Grace," said lieutenant Jack. "I think we should consolidate, scout the surrounding area looking for more survivors, while at the same time train up at least another fifty Peacekeepers, including four wagons with a couple of onagers and four scorpions. That was we'll have seventy, foot soldiers, over twenty cavalry and some serious siege busting artillery. When we've done that, we head to Charleston. After all, they had a pre-apocalypse population of around fifty thousand. Surely there must be a boatload of survivors there."

Cash leaned back in his chair. "Jack, that is one ambitious plan."

"Sorry, your Grace, I just thought…"

"No, I like it," interrupted Cash. "Just surprised to hear it coming from you. I thought you were more cautious than that."

"It's actually quite a cautious plan, if you think about it, your Grace."

"I suppose so," concurred Cash. "First things, you choose a second in command for yourself. Make him your lieutenant. Secondly, I'm promoting you to Captain. Jeb, Caleb, could you assist captain Jack?"

Both of the cavalrymen nodded.

"And bear in mind, gentlemen," continued Cash. "We got three months until full Integration. So, there is some urgency to this plan."

***

The next two months were a non-stop whirlwind of activity.

Captain Jack and Gunny put together another fifty-six Peacekeepers and sixteen artillery men to man the four scorpions and the pair of onagers. They sent to Tomahawk for more horses, both to pull the battle-wagons and for a few spares.

Once again, Sarah sent a message asking to join the new adventure, but Cash asked her to stay on at Tomahawk, under the understanding that she also travel to Redwood and Peach Hamlet to keep them both in the loop. It wasn't that he didn't think she would be a great addition to his current team, it was more that Cash valued her more to keep an eye on his capital city while he was away.

They were now a small army as opposed to a mere squad. And over time, they approached and relieved another five towns. Two of the towns did not have enough population nor infrastructure left to make them viable for upgrades. But the other three did. Cash walled them and then added his usual upgrades including interconnecting roads.

By now, he had over 3000 vassals and his System points were increasing far faster than he could spend them.

As well as that, Cash, much to his advisors' chagrin, insisted on going out alone with Bonny and seeking out high level mobs in order to grind his stats. He knew that Integration loomed large and he was determined to be as high a level as possible to face whatever came next.

The main skill that Cash concentrated on, was the control of his ax. Since the very beginning he had known that it was classed as an Elemental Weapon. This meant it was capable of using the elements of Fire, Earth, Water and Air to enhance its attack capabilities. But then he had been frustrated to find that both the level of the ax, plus his own personal level had to be high enough to take advantage of this skill.

Now, both of those levels were adequately advanced, and Cash was putting everything he had into raising them.

Initially, he had started using Lightning to enhance his attacks. It had happened more by chance than skill, and Higgins had informed him that the Lightning perk was part of the Air element.

After much experimentation, and literally hundreds of hours of battle, Cash had started using a number of simple but highly effective enhancements.

With Earth, it allowed him to do two things. Firstly, extend the length and width of the weapon. By now he could add another ten feet to its reach, and expand the width of the blades to over six feet. At the same time, he could momentarily increase the weight of the weapon. So, at the point of impact, he would add over 500 pounds of weight to the blades, enhancing its damage considerably.

Fire was self-explanatory. Super-hot flames enveloped the blades as he fought. With some concentration, he could actually project the flames for over twenty feet, but that took an exorbitant amount of mana.

Water projected a thin sheet of water some thirty feet in front of a swing. And if anyone doubted the efficiency of this perk, they only need to look at any hydraulic cutting system. Water can do some serious damage. Plus, it was good for drinking and putting out fires. Not mega-impressive, but really practical in that he could easily conjure up enough water to provide drinking for the entire army in less than a few minutes.

And finally, his favorite, Air. Lightning. Cash could project massive bolts of electricity, coat his blades with electrical energy and basically shock the fuck outa anything. He loved that perk, and as a result it was the one that had leveled up the most.

His only problem was, up until now, he had been unable to combine any of the elements. Fire and Lightning would be cool. As would Fire and Earth. But Higgins assured him it was simply a matter of practice.

Cash had also collected a number of various spell scrolls and weapons from mob drops and Boss chests. The only ones he kept for himself were the ones that pertained directly to his Cybernetic enhancements. The Power Packs. The rest he gave to captain Jack to distribute as he would. The extra loot, Cash sold, and now he had an incredibly large amount of System credits to his name. For the first time, he truly was a millionaire, and not in his fictitious Dollar exchange rate, but in actual credits.

Two months one week and five days after they had made the decision to consolidate, captain Jack, Jarvis, Jeb, Caleb and the two senior advisors of Beckley came to see Cash on one of the rare moments he wasn't out grinding.

"Your Grace," greeted Jack. "We feel that it's time. The army is as good as we can get it. We work well together; the artillery section is first class and the Peacekeepers are a well-oiled unit."

"So, you saying we hit Charleston?"

"I do, your Grace."

"Tell me, Jarvis, have your boys done much recon of the area?"

Jarvis shook his head. "A little. But as you know, your Grace, we been strung out mighty thin with taking the last five towns, integrating the local survivors and training the army. I can send a team out ahead of us. Or we could wait a few more days while they do some forward recon, bring us back the intel."

Cash shook his head. "No, it's time. Send a team ahead, tell them to watch themselves. We'll gather the army and head out tomorrow at first light. Alright, gentlemen, let's do this."

As they left the room, Cash checked out his Character Sheet, noting his recent gains and his point allocations.

Name: Cash Stone	Class: Cyberknight Level: 41	Experience Points XP 11000000 (12000000)		Hit Points HP 1400 (50) (50 per minute)	Stamina ST 1200 (40 per minute)		Mana Points MP 700 (30 per minute)
Strength 40	Constitution 36	Agility 35		Dexterity 7	Mind 37		Charisma 20
System Points 720				Credits 1200000			
Weapons – Elemental Ax – Level 15 Cybernetic crossbow – Level 10							
Perks – Personal cybernetic enhancements – Level 12 Cybernetic Armor – Level 12							
Titles – Ursine Exterminator Eager Beaver Duke Appalachia Giant Killer							
Spells – Lightning Bolt – Level 15 Healing – 8 Teleport - 7							
Companions – Bonny Stone Boss Hunter Level: 20	Hit Points HP 750 (18 per Minute)		Strength 25	Constitution 24		Agility 24	Mind 9

CHAPTER 32

Cash dismounted Stanley and stood opposite Jarvis. "Talk to me," he said.

"The whole area is a maze," said Jarvis. "It seems as though huge swathes of the city of Charleston has been razed to the ground. But then other sections are almost pristine. I mean, like pre-apocalypse untouched. Also, no Walls. My boys couldn't get closer so they aren't sure if there's water and power to those sections, but there are definitely people living there. And they look like they're going about business as usual. Trading, walking round, talking. It's seriously weird."

"Any guards or scouting groups? What about hunting parties?"

"This is where it gets even stranger," answered Jarvis. "There's all of that. But they aren't humans. They're some sort of goblin, orc things. Not sure how to describe them. Big ugly fuckers like those dudes in Lord of the Rings. Except they're more greenish than gray. Carrying basic weapons. Clubs with spikes, wooden shields. They're around eight to ten feet tall. We saw some of them hunting. They bring down their prey with nets and rocks.

Then they take them back to the humans who butcher them. Couldn't see what they do after that. But there is definitely some sort of symbiotic relationship going on there."

Cash shook his head. "Not necessarily symbiotic. I mean, that assumes some sort of mutual arrangement. Maybe the humans are enslaved. What did they look like? I mean, their demeanor. Happy? Subjugated? Beaten down? Or all, yay, here are the orc dudes, how ya'll doing?"

Jarvis raised an eyebrow. "You're right. They looked scared. And when the orc things approached them, they kept their eyes down. No real interaction."

"Like slaves," interjected Cash.

"Yep, pretty much."

"Sir, if I may," said Higgins. "Those beasts are called, Uruken. They are indeed similar to your fabled orcs. However, the Uruken are a hive type beast. They are incapable of governing themselves. Any large community of Uruken always has a hive-boss. The level of that boss will depend on the number of Uruken in the hive."

"How many Uruken you reckon there are, all in all?" Cash asked Jarvis.

The former Marine shrugged. "Hard to say, your Grace. But if I had to guess, over six hundred. Maybe even as many as a thousand. Hard to tell if there were loads more inside. Hell, I don't even know if those ugly fuckers sleep or anything."

"They do need sleep," said Higgins. "But not as

much as humans do. I would estimate that you can safely assume there are around eight hundred of them. The thing is, they will accommodate themselves in an underground warren. A series of tunnels and chambers. But you must appreciate, this is terrible news, and also extremely worrying."

"Hey, it's eight hundred low level mobs, we can take them," said Cash.

Higgins shook his head. "It's not the Uruken I'm worried about," he said. "It's the hive-boss. With eight hundred plus subjects, we are looking at a boss at a level of at least 60 to 65. Perhaps even as high as 70. There is one great advantage, albeit an outside chance at least. If you take down the hive-boss, then the surviving Uruken become almost mindless. In fact, a large number of them would simply keel over and cease living. Others would turn on each other in panic, and the few that do neither would be extremely easy to exterminate."

"Holy crap," exclaimed Cash. "So, what you saying is, we gotta chop the head off first."

"Correct, sir. But let me add that this situation is most definitely not right," stated Higgins. "In fact, I am now completely convinced that the Overlords are fucking with you directly."

Cash chuckled. "Hey, Higgins, you cussed. That's a first."

"That is because I am extremely peeved, sir," replied Higgins. "After all, there are rules. Those horrible buggers are allowed to bend them, but not to break them. The System is sacrosanct, and they have turned it into some sort of parlor game for their own amusement."

"Hey, Higgins, calm down," said Cash. "Don't sweat it, I've been peeved, as you put it, since those dickwipes fucked up my entire world. So, bending a few rules don't impress me much. Fuck them and the horse they rode in on. It's just another problem that we need to overcome. Now, let's get hold of Jack, Caleb and Jeb and work out how we gonna take this lot down."

***

As the evening sun began to dip below the horizon, Cash gathered his trusted commanders – Jack, Caleb, and Jeb – to discuss their plan of attack against the Uruken and their hive-boss. The tension in the air was palpable as they weighed their options.

"We can't just charge in blindly," Jack said, his brow furrowed in thought. "If the hive-boss is as high as level 70, we need a strategic approach. A direct assault would be suicide."

Caleb nodded in agreement. "We need to find a way to take down the hive-boss without alerting the entire horde of Uruken. If we can take him out quietly, we stand a chance."

Cash leaned against the wall, his mind racing with possibilities. "I don't think that subtlety is going to be possible here, Caleb. This is gonna be a knock 'em down grab 'em out sorta fight. Lightning, scorpions, onagers, It's gonna be big and noisy.

Caleb grinned in a slightly embarrassed fashion. "True, sorry, just thinking aloud."

"Hey, we're brainstorming here," said Cash. "There ain't no bad ideas. Except maybe that one. That was pretty crap."

They all laughed.

"Anyway," continued Cash. "We know they have scouts and hunting parties. Let's use that to our advantage. Jeb, take some of your best riders and create a distraction on the other side of the hive. Draw their attention away from the main entrance."

Jeb grinned, excitement in his eyes. "You got it, Cash. We'll ride like the wind and create chaos on the opposite side. They won't know what hit 'em."

Cash turned to Jack and Caleb. "While Jeb's team creates a diversion, Jack'll lead a small group to the entrance of the hive. Take out the guards quietly and then find a way to get to the hive-boss without being detected. Then, and this is the hard part, piss that fucker off enough to make it follow you out. Once you done that, run like hell. We gotta kite this thing to death. Caleb, I will be waiting at the entrance, as will you, the rest of the cavalry and the Peacekeepers. Jack, who's in charge of the artillery?"

"Johnson. He's a good man."

"Excellent, tell him I want everything we got

lined up and ready to rock and roll the moment Jack lures the hive-boss outa the warren."

Cash's heart pounded in his chest as the weight of the responsibility settled on his shoulders. The fate of his people and the entire region rested on their success. But he knew he had the best team by his side, and together, they could achieve the impossible.

Jack arrived back and nodded. "As soon as the diversion takes place, Johnson will set his artillery up in a semi-circle around the entrance. I've got the Peacekeepers split in two, flanking the entrance, and Caleb is gonna ready the bulk of the cavalry front and center to charge and wheel.

The plan was set into motion. Jeb and his small cavalry detachment rode off into the distance, kicking up a cloud of dust behind them as they approached the opposite side of the hive. The Uruken, attracted by the commotion, quickly shifted their attention away from the main entrance.

Meanwhile, Cash, Jack, and a detachment of Peacekeepers moved stealthily through the shadows toward the entrance of the hive. Armed with their spears, swords, and crossbows, they took down the guards silently, one by one. Cash waited to one side of the entrance, sending Bonny in with the Peacekeepers to help enrage the hive-boss to the point that it followed them out.

The element of surprise was on their side as they made their way deeper into the hive, taking out every Uruken they came across with speed and stealth.

The inside of the hive was a maze of dimly lit tunnels and chambers. The stench of decay and filth hung heavy in the air. The team moved cautiously, every step calculated, every breath held in anticipation.

Jack led his detachment of troops with silent precision, careful not to make a sound that would alert the Uruken to their presence. As they navigated the dark and twisting passages, they left subtle signs of their passage, hoping the hive-boss would sense their intrusion and follow.

Meanwhile, Cash, who had positioned himself at the hive's entrance, readied himself to unleash a massive lightning attack at a moment's notice. He knew that drawing the hive-boss out of the safety of its lair was risky, but they had to take this chance to defeat the threat once and for all.

***

Captain Jack inched forward, his six Peacekeepers and Bonny in single file behind him. They had penetrated far into the warren and had already killed over twenty Uruken. As to where the hive-boss was, it was basically guesswork. They simply followed the largest tunnels and hoped for the best.

They sidled into a huge cavern, dank and dark, it was so large they couldn't see either the sides, the ceiling, or the far end. But one thing was an assault on their senses.

The unbelievable stench.

It was like every bad smell in the world combined and then multiplied by about a gazillion. Almost a physical assault on the senses.

"Man," exclaimed Jack. "Smells like a thousand skunks died."

As he spoke, they all sensed a movement in the darkness. More a shifting of shadows as opposed to a concrete visual.

Then an eldritch light filled the vast cavern, revealing a monstrous version of one of the Uruken. The difference being that this one had massive scythe-like claws, teeth the size of spears, and it stood well over thirty feet tall.

The boss let out an ear-rending screech and stomped forward.

"Holy fucking shit on a cracker," yelled Jack. "Peacekeepers, crossbows ready, aim, fire and step back."

A volley of bolts struck the boss. But although they did manage to penetrate the monster's skin, they did little more than irritate it.

"Rinse and repeat, gentlemen," commanded Jack. "Keep firing and moving back. Watch your steps, don't fall down. Bonny, watch our six, kill any Uruken that you see."

The Peacekeepers kept moving, but instead of an orderly retreat, they had to turn and run, as the boss picked up speed. Every now and then one of them would turn and fire another bolt at the monster. At the same time, they had to clear the way in front of them.

One of the men went down as a trio of Uruken sprinted out of a concealed side tunnel, their clubs flailing as they did. They was no time to stop and attempt to heal him, and Jack used his spear to dispatch the Uruken before he turned and continued running.

The boss screeched again, and this time it tore a stalactite from the roof of the cave tunnel and threw it at the retreating group of Peacekeepers. The stone spear struck one of the men in his back, literally tearing him in half. The rest of the men redoubled their efforts in their attempt to escape.

Suddenly, they saw the light at the end of the tunnel. Another stalactite took out a second Peacekeeper, spreading his guts all over the wall and floor.

And then they were out.

But the boss was right behind them, and to make matters worse, it was being followed by a hoard of Uruken.

"Run," yelled Cash. "Keep going, draw the fucker out. Artillery, hold."

Jake, the remaining four men and Bonny sprinted out into the open, driving their legs as fast as only fear can do.

Cash waited until the boss was thirty yards out, then he cast a thunderbolt. But not at the boss. Instead, he threw the bolt at the tunnel's entrance, and with a grinding crash of thunder, the entire ceiling collapsed.

"Yes," yelled Cash. "Now you're ours, motherfucker, no escape. Prepare the crossbows and onagers!" Cash called out to his men. "Steady, everyone. We'll make our stand here and show these creatures the strength of humanity!"

The ground shook as the Uruken horde charged towards Cash and his forces. The clattering of their spiked clubs against their wooden shields reverberated through the air. But Cash and his men stood firm.

As the first wave of Uruken drew nearer, Cash gave the signal to fire. Giant crossbows and onager catapults launched a volley of deadly projectiles into the heart of the oncoming horde. The ground erupted in chaos as massive boulders and deadly bolts rained down upon the Uruken, tearing through their ranks.

The hive-boss let out a roar of fury as it witnessed the devastation wreaked upon its minions. Sensing the threat, it charged forward, its enormous club raised high in its right hand, while brandishing the huge claws of its left.

But Cash and his cavalry were ready. They rode forth, lances gleaming in the fading light. With a well-coordinated attack, they struck the hive-boss from all sides, their lances finding their mark with deadly accuracy. Foot soldiers followed, their swords slashing through the Uruken ranks.

Cash totally ignored the simple Uruken warriors, trusting Bonny to keep them off him as he concentrated solely on attacking the hive boss.

As he approached it, he used Identify.

Uruken Hive-Boss - *Level 68*
HP - *6000/6000*
Weakness – *Not much. Maybe try hitting it until it dies. Whatever.*
Strength – *Overwhelming strength. Crushing attack.*

"Great fucking info," grumbled Cash. "Aside from telling me it's a gazillion levels above me, that was no help at all."

He wound up a lightning bolt and threw it at the boss's head. It struck true and the electric charge spat and crackled as it burned into the beast's face. Screeching in anger it turned to Cash and struck out at him. Cash used teleport to move behind the boss and hit it with another thunderbolt. Then to add a bit more damage, he fired off a series of mana bolts from his crossbow.

A quick check on the boss's HP showed it had dropped to 5800 points.

"200 measly points. Shit, at this pace it's gonna take us about a hundred years to off this dickhead. We gonna need a better plan."

Cash pulled back, at the same time yelling out to Jeb and Caleb. "Back off from the boss, just try to kite it from a distance. I want the artillery to work it over as much as possible. Jack, crossbows only. Hammer this fucker and keep moving. Make sure you keep it off the artillery."

The scorpions and onagers continued to rain

destruction down on the boss, slowly chipping away at its massive HP pool. At the same time, the Peacekeepers worked at keeping the Uruken away from the artillery, while the cavalry did the same to the boss, peppering it with their crossbows.

Bonny kept Cash's six clear while he worked up another plan.

First, he used the Water enhancement on his ax, projecting a thin blade of water thirty feet in front of him as he swung. This allowed him to deliver damage but stay out of the monster's wild swing attacks. The water-blade did well. Cutting deeply enough to inconvenience the beast. But it didn't deliver enough damage to turn the battle in any way at all.

Cash threw a few more lightning bolts at the boss while thought up his next move. And after a few seconds he knew what he had to do.

It was a real Hail Mary, but at the rate they were whittling away at the boss's HP, the chances are they would eventually lose this battle. Already, six of the cavalry were down and at least eleven Peacekeepers.

Unable to accept any more casualties, Cash hefted his ax and ran straight at the boss, his cybernetic limbs driving him forward faster than a formula one racing car. At the last moment he jumped, arcing high into the air and landing on the boss's back. With a mighty swing of his ax, he hammered the blades deep into the bottom of the hive-boss's neck.

The beast went insane, screeching and flailing at Cash, but unable to reach him. Meanwhile, Cash placed his crossbow against the top of the boss's spine and fired. The proximity of the blast almost knocked Cash off his precarious hold, but he hung on like a limpet and fired again.

And again.

Then he channeled a massive charge of electricity through the blades of his embedded ax and released them directly into the boss. The nauseating stench of scorching flesh filled the air as the boss literally began to cook from the inside out.

Whenever any of the onagers or scorpions could get a clear shot that didn't put Cash in danger, they took it, continually hammering away at the boss's HP.

Bonny sprung in and out, tearing chunks off the beast's ankles and feet in an attempt to hamstring it.

As Cash's mana began to bottom out, the boss finally dropped to its knees, then, like an imploded Vegas casino, it collapsed forward onto all fours.

Cash ripped his ax out, steadied himself, raised it high and brought it down on the boss's neck. As it descended, he poured everything he had left into the Earth attributes of the weapon, draining the last of both his Mana and his Stamina. The weight of the blades increased exponentially, so when they struck, they weighed in excess of six tons.

With a sound like two locomotives colliding,

the cybernetically enhanced blades struck deep, severing flesh and bone with the mightiest of strikes.

But still, Cash couldn't fully decapitate the beast.

And he was finished. No Mana, no Stamina.

Completely and utterly exhausted.

Then Bonny jumped up and clamped her massive jaws around the boss's face. And with a savage shake of her head, she ripped it off.

True to Higgins's earlier advice, the remaining Uruken simply gave up. Some attacked their kin, others just keeled over and stopped breathing, and the rest ran.

But the cavalry rode them down and exterminated them. Crushing them like the vermin they were.

It was over.

The battle for Charleston was over.

Cash's HUD lit up like a one-armed bandit that just hit the grand prize as loads of notices flooded his vision.

He immediately dismissed them all. There would be time for that later.

He had an army to congratulate, soldiers to heal, and then a city to convince to join him.

CHAPTER 33

In the deepest recesses of the Overlord's chamber, a sense of tension hung heavy in the air. The elder Overlord, a towering figure with gray, alien-like features, seethed with anger as he glared at the holographic display before him. The younger Overlord, almost equally imposing, watched with a mixture of curiosity and unease.

"That was a level 68 boss!" the elder hissed, its voice dripping with frustration. "There shouldn't even be anything over level 50 at this stage of the game! How did he manage to defeat it?"

The younger Overlord shrugged, trying to hide its unease. "I don't know, but he's proving to be more resilient than we expected. It's almost as if the System itself is favoring him."

Its words were barely out of his mouth when the elder Overlord's eyes widened in malicious delight. "You know what? Let's escalate this. I'm starting the Integration early. If he wants to play hero, let's see how he handles a real challenge."

"Wait, are you sure that's a good idea?" the younger Overlord questioned, its doubt evident. "The System has its rules, and if we tamper with them too much..."

"Rules be damned!" the elder Overlord growled, slamming his fist on a glowing button. "I'm tired of this little cyberknight ruining our fun. Let's see how he handles the real game."

As soon as the button was pressed, an eerie silence engulfed the chamber. Alarms blared, lights flickered, and the holographic screen rippled with erratic numbers.

"What have you done?" the younger Overlord asked, its voice tinged with panic.

"I don't know!" the elder replied, fear creeping into its voice for the first time. "I've never seen this before. It's like the System is glitching, resetting, or something..."

Before they could comprehend the magnitude of their actions, a message flashed across the screen in bold, glowing letters:

System Reset.
Illegal Integration Time.
*^56$$3(#8 - read error.
Subject: Cash Stone to be Upgraded and Compensated.

The Overlords exchanged nervous glances, realizing the gravity of their mistake.

Panic and confusion reigned. The System had turned against them, punishing their unfair tactics and rewarding Cash's bravery and resilience. They realized that they had underestimated the human spirit and the power of unity.

"This can't be happening!" the elder Overlord raged, its anger giving way to fear.

"We need to fix this!" the younger Overlord urged, frantically searching for a solution.

But it was too late. The System had spoken, and there was no going back.

Cash Stone was about to be radically upgraded, and the game had changed.

And as the world trembled under the weight of their unscrupulous choices, a new chapter in the battle for humanities survival had begun.

CHAPTER 34

Cash had sent his people out in groups of ten to approach every human survivor they could find and instruct them to gather at the old College Park stadium.

As the crowd gathered at the stadium, Cash Stone stood tall before them, his presence commanding and powerful. Over four thousand people had gathered, their eyes fixed on the man who had just saved them from the clutches of the Uruken and their terrifying hive-boss. The stadium buzzed with anticipation, and Higgins, using his AI abilities, amplified Cash's voice to reach every corner of the vast space.

"My fellow survivors," Cash's voice boomed, "today marks a turning point in our struggle for survival. You have seen the power we wield, and you have witnessed the might of our small but well-trained army. But the fight is far from over."

He paused for a moment, letting his words sink in, before continuing, "I'm not going to drag this out, you all know how shitty life can be in this current RPG apocalypse. The beasts, the lack of water, power and food. Trust me, we've all been there. Plus, we only have a few more weeks until the Overlords unleash full Integration upon us, and if we're not united, we're doomed. The other races in the System will come for us, taking what's ours. We need to be prepared.

"I offer you a choice—the choice to stand with me, to take the oath as my vassals, and in return I will swear a binding oath to you. An oath to protect, to provide. And together, we shall fortify this city. I promise you power, water, accommodation, walls, and most importantly, protection. Together, as a united force, we will not only survive, but we will thrive!"

The crowd erupted in conversation, some heated, some subdued. A few people even came to blows. It was obvious that opinions were divided, with many convinced by Cash's display of strength and bravery, while others remained hesitant. Some were even adamant about not swearing any oath to anyone, regardless of the promise of protection.

Impassioned discussions and arguments continued and the minutes turned into an hour. But Cash remained patient, even though he knew that time was of the essence, they still had a few weeks, so a couple of hours wouldn't make a difference.

As the debates continued, the stadium suddenly filled with the blaring sound of a klaxon, causing everyone to wince and cover their ears.

An announcement from the System boomed out, filling the air with a sense of impending doom.

WARNING - *Integration is starting early... you have one hour to prepare.*
This is your final warning.
Integration is soon to occur.
Prepare for alien incursion and massive increase in both beast activity and levels.
Beware.
Beware.
Danger is imminent.

Panic and fear gripped the crowd, and in that moment of desperation, everyone saw the wisdom in joining forces with Cash. The prospect of facing the Integration alone was too daunting, and they knew that standing together was their best chance at survival.

With no dissent, the people agreed to swear the oath, their voices uniting as they pledged allegiance to Cash Stone and his cause. The solemn oath echoed through the stadium, sealing their newfound alliance.

"We have one hour to prepare," Cash announced. "Let's show the Overlords what we're made of. We will stand together and face whatever comes our way. As one united force, we will not only survive Integration, but we will thrive. Now, it's time for me to get to work."

But before Cash could begin the city upgrade, his HUD was inundated with messages. Unfortunately, most of it was complete gobbledygook. Random lines of code and random words combined with what looked like hieroglyphics.

After almost a full minute, the stream of figures slowed and stopped.

Then a message read –

System reboot attempt due to illegal adjustment of the System.
Subject Cash Stone.
^7&8***5$#@ error … 9**7&^6% retry …
Reboot successful.
Congratulations Cyberknight Cash Stone. You have been promoted to Archduke Stone of Appalachia.
All spells and equipment will be upgraded.
You have advanced to Level 51.
All Stats have been upgraded.
The System has allocated you 100 bonus points to allocate to Stats.
You receive 2000 System Points.
You receive the title – Cyberknight Colossus.
Congratulations, your Highness. Now, try not to fuck it up.

"Higgins, did you see that?"

"Yes, sir," replied Higgins. "I told you those bastard Overlords were gaming the System."

"That you did, Higgins," agreed Cash. "Man," he continued. "I am about to become one seriously OP motherfucker."

"Beware of overconfidence, sire," warned Higgins. "After Integration, you will find that although level 51 is more than respectable, many of the new inhabitants of the planet will be far, far higher."

"Yeah, well, fuck them," stated Cash. "Now, let's spend some System points and upgrade the hell outa this place, I got points to burn."

Even as Cash was speaking, he was selecting the upgrades – massive walls, a moat, towers, over fifty scorpions and onagers, barracks, crafting hall, accommodation, adventures guild, a greenhouse, a healing house, a System shop. And the list carried on.

Forty minutes later, the city of Charleston was complete. And it was a marvel to behold.

Seven minutes after that, the world went mad.

Sirens sounded, thunderbolts raked the earth, savage winds whistled through the city. The sky lit up like a thousand, thousand 4th of July firework displays.

Then another System message boomed across the world.

Congratulations, planet Earth, you have been Integrated.
Lay out the welcome mat and ready yourselves for visitors, for soon they will arrive.
Some will be friendly – some will most definitely not be.
But that is your problem.
Try your hardest not to die.
Live long and prosper.

System Out...

"And now the shit really starts," said Cash to himself. "I just hope I've done enough to give at least some of us a fighting chance."

He brought up his Character Sheet and, after a few minutes of contemplation, he allocated all of his points, grimacing at the fact that the System had automatically upgraded his Charisma to 30.

Then he strode off to speak to his commanders, Bonny at his side.

He had work to do.

Name: Cash Stone	Class: Cyberknight Level: 51	Experience Points XP 28000000 (30000000)	Hit Points HP 3000 (50) (100 per minute)	Stamina ST 2800 (90 per minute)	Mana Points MP 2000 (60 per minute)
Strength 65	Constitution 61	Agility 60	Dexterity 27	Mind 62	Charisma 30
System Points 2520			Credits 1000000		
Weapons – Elemental Ax – Level 25 Cybernetic crossbow – Level 20					
Perks - Personal cybernetic enhancements – Level 20 Cybernetic Armor – Level 20					
Titles – Ursine Exterminator Eager Beaver Archduke of Appalachia Giant Killer Cyberknight Colossus					
Spells – Lightning Bolt – Level 35 Healing – 20 Teleport - 15					
Companions – Bonny Stone Boss Hunter Level: 30	Hit Points HP 1500 (18 per Minute)	Strength 50	Constitution 50	Agility 50	Mind 10

****

Well, that's another chapter in Cash's quest to save as many people as he can – as well as sticking it to the Overlords.

Thanks for staying with us so far. As you

may know, I have written many books (over 40 of them), but up until this series, they have all been Urban Fantasy (And some of them have done quite well – hitting the No 1 spot in all markets). So, I'm new at this LitRPG – but hopefully I'm getting better at it.

As always – if you'd like to chat about anything, or give me some much-appreciated advice, please email me at **craig@craigzerf.com** and I promise I will get straight back to you.

Thanks again
Your friend in words

Craig

Printed in Great Britain
by Amazon